The Country Ahead of Us,
the Country Behind

*T*he *C*ountry *A*head of *U*s, the *C*ountry *B*ehind

~~~~~~~~~~~~~~~~~~~~~~~~~~~~ *stories*

*D*avid *G*uterson

1817

HARPER & ROW, PUBLISHERS, New York
Grand Rapids, Philadelphia, St. Louis, San Francisco
London, Singapore, Sydney, Tokyo

The following stories have been previously published: "Opening Day" in *Sports Illustrated* under the title "When the Hunt Is Done"; "Wood Grouse on a High Promontory Overlooking Canada" in *Washington Magazine*; "Three Hunters" in *The Iowa Review*; "American Elm" in *The Seattle Review*; and "The Flower Garden" in *Prairie Schooner*.

FIRST EDITION

Designer: Cassandra J. Pappas

Library of Congress Cataloging-in-Publication Data

Guterson, David.
    The country ahead of us, the country behind.

    Contents: Angels in the snow—Opening day—
Day of the moonwalk—[etc.]
    I. Title.
PS3557.U846C68   1989   813'.54   88-45913
ISBN 0-06-016097-7

89 90 91 92 93 CC/HC 10 9 8 7 6 5 4 3 2 1

For Robin, Taylor, Travis and Henry

Contents

1   Angels in the Snow

14   Opening Day

28   Day of the Moonwalk

43   Aliens

62   Wood Grouse on a High Promontory
Overlooking Canada

68   Piranhas

86   Three Hunters

105   American Elm

127   Arcturus

141   The Flower Garden

The Country Ahead of Us,
the Country Behind

*A*ngels in the *S*now

~~~~~~

We were at my sister's house for Christmas Eve, fire in the fireplace, lights on the tree, Christmas carols playing on the stereo. Outside the window a light snow blew down. Icicles hung from the gutters and in the yard the grass looked sprinkled with powder. By morning everything would be white.

My sister had sent her children to bed and her husband, Larry, was pouring out four glasses of champagne.

"Long life and happiness," he said, "Merry Christmas, everyone."

All this was less than a year ago.

Cora, myself, Larry, my sister: we sat around talking about normal things at first. Jobs, cars, houses, children—I don't remember exactly: pleasant conversation. But then Larry said, because my sister asked, "Christmas on Okinawa? Do you want to know what we did? We got drunk and went to sleep. We passed out. That was Christmas Eve. Christmas

Day we ate ham. We took aspirins. We called home. Some-
body at the other end yelled 'Merry Christmas!' at you.
When the echo faded you yelled 'Merry Christmas!' back.
You hung up and then you were on Okinawa again, it was
Thursday and everyone you knew had a hangover."

"Sounds great," my sister said, and kissed his chin. "What
about the Japanese hookers?"

Larry sipped at his champagne and smiled. He was a big
man in his early thirties, hands thick but not ungraceful, a
good growth of hair on his head. My sister had a way of
knocking him, of making him out to be stupid, but Larry took
it all as a joke, as harmless, as her way of loving him after
all.

Larry said, "Hey. Why not? A whore was like giving yourself a Christmas present."

We laughed at that, and in the silence that followed my
wife asked me if I had ever slept with a prostitute.

I told them how we had gone to Las Vegas, I told them the
whole story that Christmas Eve. My sister remembered—a
family vacation, Memorial Day weekend. My father'd had an
insurance convention.

"Sweet sixteen and three days in Sin City," Larry suggested, smiling. "But that's not how it was," I said. "That's not
it at all." "Well, how was it then?" Cora wanted to know. So
I told the three of them the whole thing, a mistake.

We went down there, I said. We got two motel rooms at
the end of the Strip, at the edge of town, after the swimming
pool there was only the desert, scrub brush and barbed wire
fences. It was a quiet place, hot and dusty, air conditioned,

cigarette and pop machines in all the landings. A maid came at ten o'clock and cleaned your room.

My parents went to floor shows, meetings, casinos, maybe department stores, anyway they were never around. They left us hamburger money, telephone numbers. What did they expect? What were they thinking? My sister smeared herself with suntan oil and slept by the swimming pool all day. I swam laps. I was going to be in good shape forever. The other guests lolled around while I swam furiously the backstroke and breaststroke. In the room I did sit-ups in front of the air conditioner. I looked at my muscles in the mirror. I had this *Playboy* magazine at the bottom of my suitcase. In it were photographs of Raquel Welch. Raquel in sequins. Raquel in the shower. Raquel on the beach in Mexico.

"Raquel Welch," I said to them last Christmas Eve. Was that some kind of mistake maybe? Was there something wrong in that? "It must have been *Playboy*," I said to them. "I don't remember clearly."

"He still reads that stuff," said Cora. "Not really," I insisted. "Maybe once in a while." "Oh, come on, John," said Cora. "Where're we going?" I said.

"You guys aren't going *anywhere*," said my sister. "Not at this rate you aren't."

"Not on Christmas, anyway," I said. "Tonight is Christmas Eve."

"That's the spirit," said Larry. "Peace on earth, goodwill toward men and cham*pagne.*"

He filled my glass, grinning, amused. "O Little Town of Bethlehem" played on the stereo.

"Goodwill toward *some* men, anyway," said Cora. "Goodwill is a two-way street."

"Christ," I said. "Shut up."

"Don't tell her to shut up," said my sister. "That just makes everything worse."

"You have to be *sensitive,*" Larry threw in, winking. "That's the whole thing nowadays."

"Back to Vegas," I said. "Let me *finish.*"

~~~~~~~~~~~

I was swimming laps in the swimming pool, I said. A bright day, ninety-five degrees. Up and down, back and forth, flip turns, chlorinated water sloshing in my goggles. My sister, hair in a bun pinned to the back of her head, lay sprawled out on her back like a greasy Barbie doll. Four or five others sat around in lounge chairs, drinking cans of pop and smoking cigarettes. Air conditioners dripped, a radio played, the maid rolled her cart from room to room.

I sat in the shallows. The maid wasn't half bad. She had a uniform on, like a nurse maybe. Two women lay on their breasts in chaise lounges. One had unclasped the hook to her bathing suit top. The other had a leg turned behind her; her toes made circles in the desert air. A man read a book on the far side of the pool, seated on a towel, his bald head sunburned, his pectorals drooping. By the diving board a fat man in mirrored sunglasses sat in a lounge chair looking wider than he was tall, coiling the silver hairs on his chest between his fingertips, the palm of his hand measuring the weights of his soft formless breasts.

I started swimming again—the kind of teenager who confronts boredom and the dangers of aging with a passionate, religious routine.

Back and forth, up and down, doing the butterfly, flutter

kick and slashing hands, when a room key floated down into the yellow world made possible by the lenses in my swim goggles.

"A sixteen-year-old gigolo," Larry interrupted then. "I could see it coming there, John."

~~~~~~~~

My sister had roasted some Safeway chestnuts, poured melted butter over them, sprinkled them with salt. We ate those now. We drank the champagne and cracked the shells. Larry blew out some of the candles on the Christmas tree— the ones that had burned low into their holders.

Outside, snow covered the last of the lawn. The world looked hushed, delicate and beautiful.

"A room key," said Cora. "Is that right?"

The key in the pool was the fat man's key, I told the others that evening. He waved me over when I came up with it.

I swam to where he was. I looked up and saw my face, nose like a bulb, in his sunglasses. He had his hair cut in a peculiar way—the bangs trimmed short, greasy and distinct, like a Roman soldier in a television movie.

A fat guy in a nylon bikini suit, wristwatch, black leather sandals.

"Listen," he said, leaning down toward the water. "Take that room key and go have a good time. A girl's there, she's waiting for you, big tits, a knockout."

"If this isn't fantasy, what is?" my sister asked.

But Cora said nothing. She was waiting to hear how things came out, waiting for the rest of it with her lips pressed shut.

~~~~~~~~

I told the fat man no, thank you, and left the key on the deck by his sandals.

"Room 201," the fat man said. "If you change your mind, that's where she'll be."

What was the meaning of this? I got out, hooked my thongs on, took my towel and went up to our room. Why? I asked. How much would she cost? Is this how the world of prostitutes worked? Was the fat man a pimp maybe? I felt I had connected somehow with the world of sleaze. My sister came in, took a shower, put her clothes on, her makeup. Younger than me: fifteen.

That evening we ate at a spot called "Sir Steak's," five hundred yards down the road toward town. My mother and father went to see Mitzi Gaynor. My sister read beauty magazines. I sat for a while, then went for a walk. First I went into the desert, drank a Pepsi and looked at the purple shadows of the mountains. Then, vaguely excited, I caught a bus into town.

It was all the things you've heard about. Old ladies waving keno slips. Busloads of gamblers. Drunks stumbling over the sidewalks. Neon wedding palaces. Change spilling out of slot machines.

Sixteen, alone and in Vegas for the first time in my life.

I walked down through Glitter Gulch, the middle of Vegas. I stood outside the Golden Nugget looking in. There was a Rexall Drugs, closed, a neon cowboy on a building top, a golden horseshoe suspended in midair. I sat in the lobby of the MGM Grand, hoping I would see Tom Jones, Frank Sinatra. A million cars, a million people, everyone in a hurry, everyone going to places I couldn't understand.

I wandered. I bought a Pepsi from a machine. I watched some people playing softball in a park. Moths swarmed in the floodlights. I ate a bag of barbecued potato chips, took a leak by a bush. I chewed some bubble gum and walked past the casinos. There were so many pretty girls I nearly died on the streets of Las Vegas.

That's what I told them, anyway. The truth as inspired by champagne.

~~~~~~~~~~~~~~

"His head's still turning," Cora said. "It doesn't have to be Las Vegas."

"Well, whose doesn't?" Larry said. "Name me one guy who's immune."

"Not John," said Cora. She cracked a chestnut with her fingernail. "John's got a regular rubberneck."

"Oh Christ," I said. "Come on."

"It's true," said Cora.

"Okay, it's true," I said.

My sister hit me just below the shoulder. "Will you two stop it?" she said.

"Baby in the manger and all of that," said Larry. "Cut it out, you two."

"It *is* true," I said. "My neck's made out of rubber." I dragged down the collar of my shirt to show them. "Cora's right about me."

"To hell with that," said Larry.

"To hell with what?" I said.

"You're a good enough guy," said Larry.

"I know that," I said.

"He's got eyes in the back of his head," said Cora. "He's got eyes popping out all over."

"They're just *eyes,*" said my sister. She leaned forward,

making a point out of it. "Everybody *looks,* for Christ's sake."

"That's where it stops," Larry added. "Everybody looks. But not everybody *does.*"

"That's right," I said. "Cora."

"Finish your story," she said.

~~~~~~~~~~~

I left Vegas behind. I walked back toward the motel, sweating, then caught a bus. It was all flat, it smelled of desert; the only thing standing out was the soft purple of the mountain ranges. A hot night, sultry, windless.

Big tits. A knockout. I began to imagine this.

I decided: pull out my copy of *Playboy* magazine, walk into the desert, look at the pictures of Raquel Welch and masturbate underneath the stars.

~~~~~~~~~~~

Instead I went up the stairs to the motel's second floor. I was just going to peek in the window, if I could—to get an idea of what she looked like.

"Pretty juicy, John," Larry said, filling my champagne glass again.

The curtains were pulled tight. I stood listening. I was too nervous, I guess, because the door opened then. They must have heard me panting by the window.

It was the fat man. "Glad you came," he said. He wore safari pants, a Hawaiian print shirt unbuttoned to his navel, his hairy beer gut plunging out. His small teeth looked white

and perfectly shaped. "Come in and have a drink," he offered.

"Excuse me," I explained. "This is a mistake."

The fat man pointed with his thumb at the numbers on his
door.

"Room 201," he said. "It's what you wanted, what you
came for."

At school there were girls like this one. Nobody looked at
them. Nobody noticed. I thought maybe something was
wrong with me, with the way I saw them. She was like that:
slender, tight, hair long and straight. She sat in a chair with
a mixed drink in her hand, giving off that aura of control, of
economy. An efficient, lean girl no older than twenty in a
halter top, red corduroy pants, her brown navel the center
of it all.

"This is Suzette," the fat man said. "I'm Don. You're one
hell of a swimmer. Incredible."

Whatever words I might have had to say were camou-
flaged from me. I didn't know where I was or how I'd gotten
there. It seemed as if I'd stepped outside the borders of the
life I recognized. *Don and Suzette,* I said to myself. *Names
in a porno movie.*

"To think I missed out on all this," my sister said.

"Let him finish," said Cora.

I watched Larry peel open a chestnut. The fire in the
fireplace had smoldered down to orange coals. Outside the
window the falling snowflakes looked larger, the street was
covered with a thin layer of white. At one edge of the lawn

a low drift was forming—tomorrow the children would make angels in the snow.

"You couldn't ask for better," my sister said happily. "A good snow on Christmas Eve."

I told them what happened then. I told them what the deal was. Suzette stood up with her drink in her hand. "Why don't you relax?" she said to me. "I don't know if I can," I answered. "You can," she said. "It's easy." And she came to me. She kissed me. I felt her tongue jump into my throat, her breasts, her hair falling across my cheek. "Don?" she said when she was finished. I looked up: the fat man had taken off his shirt, was working on his pants, he was stepping out of his safaris at the edge of the bed, he was naked, soft, silver and hairy, the only thing left on him was his wristwatch.

"I just want to watch," he said to me softly. "Please—don't be frightened."

"It's what he likes," explained Suzette.

"I'll pay you," Don said. "It'll work out."

Suzette took my head between her hands and kissed my cheek—flicked her tongue across it like a dragonfly. I stood there, locked up inside myself. Suzette put her fingers on the button of my shirt. She kept looking into my eyes.

"Don't be scared," she said to me. *"Please."*

Don had settled into a chair. A shine of tears lay against his pupils.

"Don't be scared," Suzette repeated.

She kissed me again, unbuttoning my shirt now. "Relax," she suggested. "Have a good time."

I got out of there. I don't know how, exactly. I only know that when I found myself again I was in one of the landings leaning against an electric icemaker.

"Boo," Larry said. "Oh, come on! I was *sure* you were going to get laid there, John."

I said, "In answer to your question, Cora, that's the closest I've ever come to having sex with a prostitute."

But when we went up to bed she wouldn't speak to me or look at me.

"What is it?" I said.

"You," Cora whispered.

I didn't know what that meant. So I asked her to explain.

Cora lay on the bed in her nightgown, speaking to the ceiling, to the darkness. "You're driven by *sex,"* she said. "Do you know what I mean? Do you know what you're made of? What made you go up to that motel room anyway? Can you answer without lying to yourself, to us?"

"I was sixteen," I complained.

"Sixteen," she answered. "That's a lie. Sixteen—that doesn't explain anything."

"I got out of there, didn't I? Before anything happened? Didn't I get out of there?"

"You were young," she said. "You just said that."

She pounded the mattress with an open palm, turned away, looked through the bedroom window, where snow hung gently falling against the darkness. "What would you do *now?"* she asked. "You don't even have to answer that."

"I never would have been there in the first place," I said.

"That's a lie," said Cora.

"Why would I lie?"

"Because you always do. And you never admit it. That's what's really *sleazy."*

She cradled one cheek in the palm of her hand, as though she was reading a book in bed, and stared at the snow beyond the window. Her hair, I remember thinking, was why I had married her—black hair, a lot of it.

"It's a lie," she said. "Sixteen—that doesn't explain anything. I know who you are, John, better than you do. I see it in you all the time, everywhere we go."

"Cora," I said. But there was nothing to follow it up with. Because I knew what she was talking about. I knew exactly what it was. I knew the thing inside me she was pointing to.

I lied. I lied to her even though it was Christmas. I didn't want to tell her about where I'd been and what I'd been, even though somehow she already knew about it. She could *feel* it; it sprang from me like some bad odor. But it was easier that way, I decided just then—easier to leave it like that than to talk about it, so I lied. It was a perfect opportunity not to, maybe, but I lied because it was easier. I said, "I was young then. It doesn't have anything to do with me now. I've grown up. I'm a different person."

~~~~~~~~~~~~~~~~~

The next morning the world was a fragile, white place, the branches of the spruce trees loaded down with snow, the wind blowing cold and the sun dazzling, the children opened their gifts, screaming, we went outside and threw snowballs in the yard, ate a pleasant supper, drank buttered rums, it was all a joke, the story forgotten, Christmas usurping everything else.

We made angels in the snow, Cora and myself, swept our arms through the powder, left an impression of wings that would melt before the new year.

What happened? I often ask myself that. There was a chain of things, I guess, long and confused, so that even I can't unravel it. The last one, we were at somebody's party. I was in a swimming pool. Kissing a woman in the shallows. We both had our clothes on, mostly. I was too drunk. After that, Cora was gone.

Opening Day

~~~~~~

We waited for morning in a sad little motel where you could smell hunters skulking in every direction. I lay listening to vague presences in the next room, strangers playing lonely rounds of five-card draw, until it seemed all right to dispense with the minor pretense of the clock and, gently, wake up my father and son. Pop couldn't turn himself over or sit upright first thing; he wheezed once and guessed he didn't want to be spry; everything hurt and it was no use pretending otherwise. But Sean, yawning, made a clean break from his dreams, spun from the bed, wheeled toward the bathroom, and after he had let loose a brash stream of night water, sprawled like a prince on his motel pillows stuffing shells into the pockets of his field jacket. "Come on, Pop," he said. "Up and at them."

Pop grunted, blinking, and fished for his glass of teeth, words leaking from the corner of his mouth, sour ire. "You thlow down, Thawn. Take afther your damn dad. Tho damn frithky firth thing like that."

I shook my head: they were both immoderate. "That was a long time ago," I reminded Pop. "Besides, any other morning you couldn't roust Sean out with anything short of TNT."

Pop fixed his teeth in place. "Not so long," he said, trying them out, his jaw working them over, the long crevices in his cheeks churning. "Where are we going to get breakfast?"

We drove through a silent and frosted darkness with the sage desert just beyond the pale of the road. Along the strip of autumnal, shameless motels, hunters loaded gear in lots lit by running lights, steam spewing from their mouths. The dogs circling just beyond the tires, the bald fences enclosing vacant guest pools, the last of the good willow leaves, the distant odor of the slaughterhouses, neon, all beneath lonesome heavens. "What did we forget?" Pop wondered aloud. "There's no Seven-Eleven in this sage desert." Everybody, all the businesses, had thrown themselves open at four o'clock in the morning, small pools of comforting light at the verge of Moses Lake, hawking last-minute wares. Faint in the west, toward the dark mountains and home, a loose, silky band of clouds wandered the long route of the horizon— Pop pointed them out to us readily. "We'll get flurries at noon," he predicted. "It just might help."

At breakfast we inhabited a world solely of hunters, some of them in camouflage, all of them interested in eating swiftly, most of them younger than myself it seemed, though not as young as Sean, and most of them waxing and waning through a studied, dark calm that belied an unspeakable eagerness. Pop tried to give away his pancakes three or four times before Sean took them off his hands uncomfortably. "You need them," Pop explained. "Eat them up. Go on, son."

"You sure?"

"Sure I'm sure."

"Keep half."

"Don't want half."

"You'll be hungry later."

"Take them." Pop pushed the plate away with his knife blade. "Now eat them up. Go on."

He watched without concealing the pleasure he took in it: an unbridled appetite was something he celebrated, for better or for worse. Sean, oblivious, clenching the tines of his fork between his big teeth, drowned everything in warm maple syrup.

Pop, with his pipe lit, had the waitress fill his thermos with sugared coffee for the day ahead. On the way out we found the tight foyer wedged with hunters, and in the parking lot more were adjusting their caps and talking to their dogs beneath the lights. "Smell that sage," I said to Sean. "It's the strongest smell you've got out here. It's everywhere."

"Some sage'll live for a hundred fifty years," Pop reflected. "Same sage Chief Joseph smelled, you're smelling now."

"Smells good," Sean said. "Let's get out into it."

I drove out on Dodson Road. To the left, desert, to the right, irrigated wheat fields under a heaven of cold stars. Canoes were putting in where the road crossed the wasteway. The sidelots were filled with stirring hunters, campers, vans, trailers, pickup trucks, lantern lights in curtained windows. Some, distant phantoms, had already set off into the desert with their flashlights wavering at their sides. The autumn wheat had been threshed down to stubble, but still stood high enough for birds to lie in; they would run in front of you in fields like this, refusing to put up unless they had to. "A lot of grain out there," Pop noted. "Sunny weather's been good to these wheatmen." We passed a lone pintail set down on a gutter pond. "They've got about an hour and a half left to do that," Sean said, swiveling to watch as we passed by.

We pulled off at the gate and began to parcel out the decoys. Pop couldn't seem to get his load just right; Sean held the light for him while he made it up slowly, a burlap sack and two pack straps of manila cord, the same rigging he'd employed for more than fifty hunting seasons. We picked up our weapons, I dragged low the top strand of barbed wire beside the gate and the three of us stepped over the range fence into the sage desert, following the twin ruts of a fading cattle road.

"Trail gets worse every year," Pop said. "No cattle in it anymore."

Sean said, "You don't need a trail out here, though. Just make a beeline for the wasteway."

"Trouble with that is a bee don't have to walk. He doesn't get sand in his boots."

A quarter-mile in, Pop's load went; it sprang away from his back without warning and flopped down into the bunch grass. We waited while he got his knots just so, Sean gouging the sand with his boot heel and weighing the shells in his pockets. I was overdressed and heating up quickly, so I unbuttoned my jacket and took off my cap. The three of us hiked through chickweed and Johnson grass. The sky had already gone from black to purple when Pop pointed out the morning's first birds—a flight of mallards wheeling toward the northwest, eleven or twelve in silhouette. "They're coming in from The Potholes," he told us, following their sleek dip and swerve. "Those birds are definitely looking for a place to set."

"Let's get up there," Sean said. "Come on."

He moved on ahead of us. Pop and I sat against the base of a sand bluff for a while.

"How's the knee? Bothering you?"

Pop rubbed once or twice beside the outside tendon. "Not too bad. Not yet."

We followed a ridge, conjuring everywhere the bustle of pheasants in the sage. We climbed over a black dune, worked down to a section marker, then crossed between two pieces of cattail marsh where for years we'd gotten creditable jumpshooting just by splitting up and combing the shallow margins. Pop had put in plenty of good days here; I'd watched him get a triple more than once. I was driven to recall a flight of mallards that got up in the south pond, scattering, twenty years ago, Pop taking a left and then a right and at the end, incredibly, a going-away. I wondered if he remembered it. If all the ducks and even the upland hunting faded together in his brain.

It was light enough to move without the flashlights now. Strands of honkers, broken Vs, skated past darkly a thousand feet overhead. It didn't matter how many times you witnessed them in flight, their speed, their unity of purpose, their impressive altitude, the faint but audible sound from fifty throats—it left you with a pounding in the rib cage. Pop watched them, too, from under his pack load. I could hear him breathing. We traversed the last black dune side by side, slowly, and stood gazing out across the wasteway.

"There it is," Pop said. "Damn."

Marsh reeds, golden cattails, pockets of gray water for as far as you could see north and south. The sage desert, impossibly large, rolled away to the east and behind. While we watched a string of teal angled in, just where we'd had our set so many years. We heard shooting, first shots of the day, a teal plummeted like a ball of coal, and soon, shooting from every quarter.

"We're a little late," I said. "It's open season."

"What happened to Sean?"

"Getting into his waders."

"Channel moves further out every year. Deeper, too."

"We can lay our set this side of it, Pop. No reason to try and cross."

We scrambled out a point of sedge and worked our waders on. Sean had his things beneath a thorn willow, neatly. "Let's go," he said to us. "Come on."

I let him lead. Bunched tight we followed the bracken margins, hip high a quarter-mile or so, going laterally with the pull of the wasteway. We were in it, guns aloft. You could feel it sucking against the backs of your waders. I watched while a pair of trout shot away, more silently than in dreams I'd once had of them, moving in tandem toward the reeds.

Pop found us a dependable set—high marsh just upwind, good drift, thick bracken; we anchored the decoys at the low end, down current but well out in the open. It was belly-high work to get them placed so I did the deep wading myself. Pop had his pipe lit and stood in the reeds, tossing the decoys out to me; then each of us took up a twenty-yard stretch and faded into the camouflage.

The first ducks came in before an hour had gone by; there had been shooting everywhere, and now it was our turn. They were mallards, a group of four wheeling over too high to be heard, jumping across from the wheat fields having fed beneath the stars, and skittish because all the familiar places swarmed, this day, with the echoes of desperate gunshots. I beckoned them first with a feeding call, a series of low, gradual chuckles, and then with the harsh cry of hen to drake. They circled twice, wide arcs in order to cover the high reeds to the north; on the third pass all four set their wings beautifully and rode in with the wind bucking them up a bit. I saw them fluff up their breast feathers; there was some splashing confusion about the decoys. Sean stood in and took the lead bird with a close wing shot, and I took a hen going away to the left. She zagged once, then plummeted head over heels with her wings folded up, propelled away from me for a half-second, no more, by the violent thrust of the shot. The two remaining singles veered off climbing powerfully; Sean wasted a second shell on the hind one.

"Yours is swimming," Pop called from his blind. "Go on, son. Finish what you started."

Sean sluiced his wounded drake, looking sheepish, I thought, and reloaded afterward on the spot. We let the two birds drift out past the decoys until in the end they were awash against the cattails.

"Can I go around and pick them up?" Sean called. "I want to see how big mine is."

"They aren't going anywhere," Pop answered. "Leave them be, why don't you?"

The battle went forth all around through midmorning; hunters were gunning away at the high flyers, and Pop cursed them once or twice. Nothing would come down in this rain of steel shot; the ducks were going to stay skittish. I tried calling in a stray set of teal, but they weren't falling for it and scurried away over the bluffs. Everything else was dumbfounded high flyers.

Then at noon, sure enough, we got the winds Pop had prophesied, and suddenly, funneling low and hugging the terrain, no fewer than thirty teal passed through our set with their wings drumming the air above the water, a whole flurry of them, dark and flashing, and nobody getting a shot off but Sean, who emptied his gun at them to no avail. They peeled off to the east with a unified grace, climbing in a long bank of silhouettes, until distance erased them from sight.

"What happened?" Sean asked.

"Caught me sleeping," I said. "They were moving too fast. I never got shouldered."

"Working on my pipe," Pop called out. "Damn!"

When the air teased down a bit we stood out for lunch — sliced beef sandwiches, a wedge of pie each. Pop lit his pipe and held his knee in his hand. The sun had come up strong over the desert—bad for hunters, but pleasant at lunchtime. We opened our jackets and passed the water around, cold and tinted with the canteen taste. Pop watched while Sean lit into his pie, and so did I, pouring from the thermos.

"I wonder if we shouldn't try some jumpshooting," Sean said. "Maybe that'll be the ticket."

"Better not wander," answered Pop, sipping coffee. "Some of these skyshooters might mistake you for a stray and try to pot you in the brush."

"There's ponds over yonder." Sean pointed toward the southeast. "Nobody's shooting down that way. Singles have been going in all day over there. The strays get confused and end up along the margins. I'll bet we get some shooting down there. I'll bet we do, Pop."

"How much?" asked Pop. "You might and you might not. But you go ahead and find out, why don't you?"

"With three of us we just might get one up."

"You can do it just as easy with two, boy."

Sean and I tracked down a nice string of ponds to walk,

and I took another mallard hen going off on the diagonal. She had trouble gaining altitude and gave me plenty of time to establish my lead and squeeze off without relying on instinct. I did it all in my head, which was satisfactory enough. She tumbled, a blur of feathers, and splashed behind the reeds. I let Sean go in to pick her up.

We walked a mile and a half of sage; there were no birds anywhere and it seemed just as well. Sean had his eye out for ringnecks, I could tell, though he knew they were impossible to flush without a bird dog. But he was very young, only twenty.

Finally we sprawled on the highest of the black dunes. Here you could see the whole length of the wasteway, its pools of sunlight, its matted rush, glistening down toward the Saddle Mountains.

"We're not getting the shots," Sean said, lying back with his hands behind his head. "I hate a slow day. I really do."

"It's good just being out," I reminded him.

"You know something? Pop hasn't fired a shot all day. You'd think he would've by now."

"He's shot his share over the years, Sean."

Sean pumped a shell loose and blew sand from it. "Still," he said. That was all.

"He'll get a shot before the day's out," I predicted. "We all will. At twilight."

Heading in we worked the margins of the wasteway together, cutting up the bracken quietly. I remembered what Pop said about the shallows on a busy day: because flight had proved itself too precarious, strays holed up and refused to bounce out unless you nearly stepped on their tail feathers. I figured if they flushed it would be with the wind under them, so we spread and beat the edges with the breeze in our faces. Sure enough a pair of pintails towered, and Sean took them both, a head-on and a going-over. They were good shots and he gave a shout when the birds fell, holding his twelve-gauge aloft.

We brought the three birds in and retrieved our two drifters from where the current had pinned them to the reeds. Sean thrust his pintails up for Pop to see, and Pop answered by raising his pipe above his head.

Gusts came up again in the late afternoon. I stood in with Pop to keep him ready, knowing he would sit on the bracken when he tired. "Where was it we got our Christmas goose?" he asked. "I believe it was down toward the reservoir from here. Just this side of those big bluffs."

"It was back that way. The twin ponds. Up underneath where the butte bulges."

The first of the blackbirds began to work now. Solitary pairings, gliding after insects, then clouds of them, wave after wave, undulant and synchronized, like schools of fish. They dropped steeply, then banked, spun in a whirlwind, exploded toward the twilight heavens. Mallards began to move in flurries. A pair circled, once, twice—their arcs enormous, elongated coils—then set from behind, so that we had to take them late, a drake and a hen dropping in from over the shoulder, two rough going-away shots in the end. I left the lead bird for Sean and told Pop to let fly, but he hesitated and Sean missed altogether; they banked and whirled on a fortunate draft and we had no birds to show for it.

"Mark," Sean called out. "They're coming out of the woodwork now."

A lone mallard hen, skimming low, nearly set among our decoys before Sean fired at her—neatly and with the proper composure. It was a rare display of patience on his part, I thought, but he missed at any rate and she veered over the cattails, skimming still, before he dropped her cleanly with a long second shot. He was still reloading when a group of eight began to circle the upwind reeds, turned away as if to give it up, then coiled back again, suspicious, circling twice more and then angling in uncertainly, pulling up at thirty yards and stroking hard over our blinds; I fell back in the bracken and squeezed off at a going-over without giving her the proper lead time and the eight of them soon cleared gun range.

"Call them in!" Sean screamed. *"Mark!"*

I gave out with the feeding call, as anticipatory as any boy, for it seemed to me, with the coming darkness inevitable, that these would be the last birds of the day. They were green-winged teal, two dozen or more, listing to the right and approaching on a low slant, a tight flock swift in flight but apparent from far off, so that I had time to remind Pop to get shouldered and fire when I did. When they dropped precipitously against the wind I knew Sean would hold himself; then they were settling down on the water, then trailing up away from the still decoys with their wings bucking, breasts opened, then floundering in slow motion over little splash pockets on the pond, tails dripping quicksilver, and I stood in and fired with perfect ease. Sean put two birds down, firing too quickly in succession when he had time— missing on the second shot—but I took a triple with the kind of slow deliberation I have found myself in recent years capable of. I have no quick shot any longer.

"Nice shooting," Pop said, with his hand on my arm. "You did it just like I would have. Pretty as a picture shooting."

In the final light I hauled out our decoys and wrapped their anchors, and my son collected, on the drift, the six birds still on the water. I didn't ask my father why he hadn't shot, but Sean did, with the blind ease of youth. "I don't lead so well," Pop told him. "It's just opening day. I'm a tad ragged, I guess. I can't get onto them yet."

But we had plenty of birds, eleven for the day; things felt right and it had been a perfect hunt. I let Sean carry them strung and draped over his shoulders, and I knew—or rather, know—what illusory thing he felt wading. Pop sloshed along behind us with his burlap bag across his back and his pipe clutched between his front teeth. "Beginning to get cold," he said once.

The day reversed itself; it was dark again and, freed from our waders, guns emptied of shells, we sojourned back across the sage and black dunes. Sean explained to Pop how he'd come by his pintails, how with the head-on the barrel of his gun had temporarily obscured the bird from sight, how with the going-over he'd swiveled and planted to take him nearly on the going-away. Chains of geese reeled overhead. The blackbirds had settled in for the night. When the first stars came up a coyote began to cry; I stopped to listen, smelling the sage, and Sean left me in his boot tracks. He went off with all the birds over his shoulders and his flashlight broadcasting across the sagelands.

Pop limped up behind and we sat down. "Knee," he said. I gave him my canteen; we rested in silence. "Down in there," I said, pointing below us, "are the ponds where you got that good triple jumpshooting. It was the south pond. Nineteen sixty-five, I believe."

Pop, wiping his lips with the back of his hand, only nodded blankly and returned the canteen. But I could see that he remembered.

"It's kid's stuff to live for that sort of thing," I told him.

I had to pull him up because he didn't want to rise on his own. I stayed behind him now. I watched his back, the burlap sack, the way he picked his knee up gingerly and kept the weight from his left leg. We sat every so often. "Damn sage," Pop said. "It just sort of fills you up."

I didn't know what to say. So I said nothing. If anyone should have had words for him then it would have been me, but I couldn't think of any.

Near the end we were hardly moving. "We're at the coot ponds," I pointed out. "It's not more than two hundred yards to the fence." But we sat for a long time in the sand, saying nothing. I could see that my son had the headlights on. "Just a few more steps," I said to Pop. "Come on."

"You go on ahead," he answered. "I'll get there sooner or later."

"You sure?"

"I want to just sit here for a while."

I went ahead and waited with Sean. On the truck's hood, one by one, we laid the ducks out and looked them over. The teal had buffy undertail coverts; one of the mallards had the tightest curl of tail feathers either of us had ever seen. "Not a bad opening day," Sean said. "Eleven birds. Count them."

He kept running his flashlight over them. "Meat for the table," he said. I wanted to tell him how wrong he was, how meat for the table was a boy's illusion, but I didn't because I knew that quite soon enough he would find it out for himself.

At last Pop was at the barbed wire. "All right," he said firmly. "Let's get out of here."

He slept as we drove back across the mountains, slept like a baby with his chin against his chest after dinner at a

roadstop in Vantage. Sean slept too and I crossed Snoqual-
mie Pass on my own, alone with my thoughts. There was
snow at twenty-five hundred feet but the semis had it
cleared from one lane nicely and I followed their track over
the summit with the wipers barreling and the defroster roaring in my ears. At North Bend Pop perked up and, pipe lit
again, sat with his head against the side window.

"What is it?" I said.

"Nothing."

We crossed the floating bridge into Seattle. Sean woke up,
wiped his eyes with his knuckles and looked around at the
rainy streets. "We're back," he said. "Damn, Dad."

"You can't hunt every day," I told him.

Then when I pulled up in front of Pop's apartment building I began to understand his silence. I opened up the back
of the camper and hauled out his burlap sack with its waders, thermos and field jacket inside. It smelled powerfully of
sage, and when I looked in I found the sprigs of it he'd
collected for his living room.

Everyone shook hands all around and a lot of things were
left unsaid. My father didn't want to take any of the birds;
didn't want to draw and pluck them, he said. I walked him
down the corridor and got him inside; Pop limped away and
started up the bathwater.

Settling in beside my son again, turning the key in the
ignition, it came to me what Pop had left behind. The engine
hadn't caught before Sean noticed it, too, and he turned to
me for a resolution. "Pop's gun," he said. "He forgot it."

I put my hand on his forearm. "Go on and take it into
him," I almost said, but I didn't, I stopped myself, and the
two of us drove away from there. My son didn't say another
word.

Day of the Moonwalk

*I*n the summer of 1969, while playing a game of basketball, my brother Harold blew out his knee. For some time afterward he walked with crutches, then with our newly dead grandfather's cane, and finally with a pronounced limp that faded until, to everyone in our family but me, he appeared to have made a complete recovery.

In July of that year—the summer of the moonwalk; the summer when I fantasized about playing for the Lakers and being Jerry West or Elgin Baylor—our family sojourned from Seaside, Oregon, where my parents were managers of a small, sand-wracked motel, to a north Seattle neighborhood of new-built homes, many of them in varying stages of incompleteness, some mere foundations or yawning craters in the earth, some framed up but still skeletal, without roofs, others half-plumbed but not wired, or vice versa—the line of houses on our side of the block was a stark and vivid frieze about the growth of cities, and wandering through them at the age of thirteen I felt the disquieting security of having so many unpossessed places to hide, as if the furtive corners of these half-built, lifeless homes could be counted on in times of darkest trouble, if they came somehow; for times of trouble—poisoned water in the tap, unformulated enemies, hydrogen bombs dropping from the Seattle skies—seemed always just ahead to me for some reason.

Coming up from Seaside in the back of our Bel Air, I listened to Harold recite the names of all the presidents in order, ending with Richard Milhous Nixon. His ability to perform this feat was vaguely irritating to me; when we'd cleaned motel rooms on summer afternoons he'd often muttered the names of presidents under his breath while exhorting me to work with greater energy so that the two of us could be done with it sooner. Today Harold is a pediatrician, a soft-spoken man of thirty-five with the emaciated limbs and astonishingly thin face of an Auschwitz survivor— one of those stick figures that stares at you from black-and-white photographs of the Holocaust as if to say: *I am alive, but just barely.* I sometimes ponder how it must be for children to have Harold tapping at their bony chests, if he is an adult who engenders in them fear or trust, if his hands inspire confidence or not. He never married. At fifteen, that summer his knee went, he was aggressively and obnoxiously competitive, an adrenalated whirlwind when it came to games of any sort; he was, in his own stringy, blue-eyed, determined way, unbeatable at just about everything.

While Harold named presidents beside me in the backseat I watched intently the passing landscape, nervous that our father might be too inept as a driver to get us all safely to Seattle. I'd seen him, only hours before, fumble with backing up the U-Haul trailer that now flew along behind us like a ponderous shadow, carrying everything our family possessed in its gloomy, malodorous insides. My mother, her bare feet propped just over the glove compartment, read *Woman's Day* magazine from behind her sunglasses, a straw hat pulled down over her head, her thick hair braided down her spine. My father listened to a Pacific Coast League ball game—Portland vs. Spokane? Portland vs. Tacoma?—on the Bel Air's fading radio, one index finger wrapped around the bottom of the steering wheel, the back of his shaved neck—from where I sat—sunburned and latticed with pale crevices. He wore his hair cropped short and gelled rigorously with Brylcreem, a Hawaiian print shirt, zoris, and his bathing suit, below which his slack thighs lay pale against the car upholstery. He was much given to rooting in his nose as he drove and, at crucial moments in the baseball game, turning up the radio volume to deafening levels. At these times Harold fell silent.

"Twenty questions," our father said, just before Astoria, because he felt we were bored and that he owed us something. "Let's see which one of you can get it, all right?"

"Male?" said Harold.

"Yes."

"Before nineteen hundred?"

"Yep."

"American?"

"Right."

"A president?"

"Right."

"Abraham Lincoln?"

"No."

"George Washington?"

"You got it."

Harold clapped his hands emphatically. "I did it in six," he pointed out. "Did you hear that, mom? I did it in six."

"Very good," said our mother.

In such a manner we flew north together, in our box on wheels, dragging our possessions behind us. We all knew how momentous this journey was: when my grandfather died in heart surgery that spring my mother came into a modest inheritance, and with this my parents made the down payment on the Seattle house, for they desired, the two of them, a new life in the city, the life they had talked about for many years. In Seaside they'd grown weary of vacuuming sand from ravaged motel rooms while the wind from the Pacific blew seams into their faces and made them both old before their time. They'd wanted to be free of this wind and sand and of empty wine bottles on bedside tables and of living like visitors in the motel's office-apartment while strangers came and went ceaselessly, leaving behind an eternal mess to be cleaned up so that others could come along and, finding it clean, wreak havoc on everything because they deigned to. They were tired and wanted to be where cleaner jobs were and where my mother's family was; they took it for granted that moving to this new place meant all things unwanted could be left behind, and they persisted, for years to come, in believing that they could always move again should their lives begin to turn sour on them. We have all thought this, people have always thought it; but this fact did not prevent the idea from taking root in my parents' hearts and nurturing them through all the harsh times.

We crossed, in our Bel Air, the gray-green breadth of the Columbia. We passed through Megler, Naselle, Raymond, Artic, Melbourne, Montesano, Elma. And as the journey thickened and the towns became more foreign to us we all became less talkative—each with our private universe of sentiment to contemplate en route to a new home to live in. We watched the world rush past outside our windows and felt that it was increasingly alien, increasingly strange but beckoning.

Now, if a move to a new place is an opportunity for change in whom we have thus far played at being, then all of us, traveling north together, must have noticed the expectant quiet that seemed to me to settle over the land as the Bel Air rolled up Highway 12, drawing us with it toward a new life in which—because we were only human, a human family—the passions that had thus far held us together might be forever rearranged under the sky of a distant city.

It was the day before Neil Armstrong walked on the moon—presumably with the good of all mankind as his purpose—that my family arrived in Seattle. My father, his elbow slung out the Bel Air's windowframe, gave the rest of us a running commentary. "Space Needle," he said perfunctorily. "Site of the '62 World's Fair . . . Husky Stadium over there . . . Green Lake off to the left somewhere." He fumbled his way off the interstate, our trailer pitching along behind. For a while we rambled along a wide boulevard, then over narrower, newer streets through rows of placid ranch houses, finally past a claustrophobic, overpaved city park. "See that basketball court?" said our father, proudly. "The lights come on at night out there. The net's made out of chain links. And it's just three blocks from your new house."

Harold and I both looked at it; or rather, I spied on Harold while he looked through the window at the basketball court our father had pointed out.

"Looks pretty good," he observed.

The winter before, in Seaside, we'd stood on the concrete at the elementary school and took turns shooting thousands of free throws together, steam spewing from our mouths. My brother began his shot from the center of his belly, his mouth hung open, his elbows tucked in, utterly dependent on some physical inner rhythm that would allow him, at the right moment, to release the ball. It was a thing of beauty, I see now. With the snow shoveled aside so that a lane to the basket was cleared, and icicles plunging from the school-house eaves, he made ninety-six in a row one afternoon, his eyes glassy and still in his face, his fingers numb, saying nothing. His rhythm was exacting, impeccable, but anxious. These minutes of shooting a basketball in the cold were fraught with a deep dread of missing. On that afternoon I stopped shooting my own shots and became his personal rebounder. I felt his rhythm right from the beginning and fed it with a precision no one else could quite *get.* There was an unspoken agreement between us on this: I would sense how he needed the ball in his hands, and when it should arrive, and how gently it must assert itself; he, for his part, would put the ball in the basket.

In this manner—together—we progressed to the 1969 Oregon Free Throw Tournament. My brother's name appeared in the Portland papers: twenty-five out of twenty-five in the semifinal round: *steely perfection at fifteen,* wrote a reporter for *The Oregonian.* In the finals, at halftime of a U. of Portland game, he missed one only because I threw it to him wrong: it was his final attempt after twenty-four in a row had slipped through the cords impeccably. The ball caromed off the back of the rim, bounced straight up and disappeared behind the backboard—crazily, embarrassingly, extracting a groan from the gathered crowd. He won anyway, and his trophy stood on a bookcase in our family's house for many years to come.

Watching him scrutinize the court near our new home I wondered if he would shoot free throws there in the same manner; if everything, in short, would be the same here. Perhaps Oregon had not been enough for him; perhaps he would need Washington State, too.

When we turned onto our new block finally two boys were in the street, tossing a baseball back and forth. The neighborhood, with all its half-built homes, had the chaotic aspect of a war zone. Shirtless men shingled the roof of one house while a cement truck churned, pouring concrete across the way. The dirt had a scabbed and ravaged appearance—you had the feeling that the earth was being remade on an impossibly titanic scale. Bulldozers had gouged our street out of blackberry riots to make room for exactly eighteen homes. In the end all would come to look egregiously similar; fronted by squares of immaculate lawn, guarded by yard lamps that blinked on at twilight, the split-level facades of our neighborhood were like sad, gaping and embarrassed faces set in the sill of the earth. In silhouette, on summer evenings, men mowed the grass or washed automobiles— but no one *knew* anyone. The place suggested somehow a necessity for distance, and thus on that first day—before the neighborhood existed, really—there was no one to greet us first of all, and no will to greet us even if there had been, as we did not greet those who followed us there out of the unformulated conviction everyone shared that one's neighbors would inevitably move on.

My father pulled cautiously into the drive of our new home: "This is it, guys," he said. We spilled out onto the sidewalk together; my mother, producing a key from a chain around her neck, ceremoniously unlocked the front door. Then all of us wandered through the vacant rooms together, the freshness of things inspiring in us a brand of reverence—"Don't touch the walls," said my mother. Our voices echoed in the empty, painted chambers, alien, unsettling sounds. In astonishment we stood at the threshhold of our dining room. An imitation chandelier, festooned with vaguely absurd cut-glass diamonds, hung by a chain from the ceiling. In the bathroom two sinks had been set in the tile; the wings of the mirrors swiveled on chrome hinges and the cabinets were stained with linseed oil. We inspected the kitchen together. My mother operated the garbage disposal; my father slipped the brass bolt in the Dutch door. We admired the counters and the window sills and closets. It seemed that some diminutive empire had been created for us, bordered by fences and careful rockeries, to close out that other world of wind and sand from which we had recently emerged together.

"We have to celebrate," announced my father. "We'll bring everything in first, then eat, have a party." He backed my mother against the kitchen sink, hoisted her up and turned her in a circle; her heels flew out behind her. "I should have carried you across the threshold," he said, snapping his fingers. "What was I thinking of?"

"It's not too late," my mother told him.

He carried her across, of course. It must have seemed to

him then that the life he had dreamed of was within reach. How was he to know then what he would have to bear? That my mother would die of lymphoma twelve years later? That they would sell this new house within five years? That he would sit by her in the hospital and wish for an end to it all?

That night, since we had no beds yet, Harold and I slept on the living-room floor—or rather *didn't* sleep because the place was too strange, the house too noxious with fumes of paint, the night too sultry, too windless. I'd always slept in the same room with Harold and had carried this tradition with me to the new place. But it occurred to me now that I didn't have to. In the new place there was a bedroom for everyone.

"You think things are going to be different here?" I said.

"Some things," said Harold. "Sure they are."

"Like what?" I asked. "Name something."

Harold turned onto his back beside me. We'd stripped to our underwear, and lay facing the ceiling with our hands behind our heads, our elbows pointing out like wings. The light from a streetlamp gathered in the window and swarmed across Harold's tightened rib cage and over the as yet untainted plasterboard. "Like a lot of things," he answered. "I don't know."

"I'm *glad* I'm going to have my own room," I told him. "I can do whatever I want now."

We were silent for some time. It was the kind of silence that often follows insult, when no one is quite certain of the meaning of silence—a nervous interim, even between brothers.

"That's fine," said Harold, after a while. "Fine."

"It has to be," I told him. "So *there.*"

He slept after a while. I didn't. I never slept as well as

Harold did, and still today I seem always to be restless when others have slipped into the world of dreams.

~~~~~~~~~~~~~~~~

It was the day of the moonwalk, a thing that seemed to us more distant than the moon; while planets disintegrate and stars are born we migrate, love, make plans, pare our fingernails, hate one another ceaselessly.

Before ten o'clock that morning Harold and I were at the basketball court our father had pointed out to us.

"Shoot for outs," he said.

"You shoot."

"First one to make it."

"You go first."

Harold shot. It went in, naturally, a swish.

"By ones to fifteen," said Harold, after I missed. "Win by two, make it–keep it."

"Take it out," I said.

I gave him the ball. He tucked it under his wiry forearm and smiled at me with what I took to be an underhanded beneficence.

"Good luck, brother," he said to me.

He drove to his right, turned his back to the hoop, and committed himself to that subtle chess match all basketball players know about: maneuvering toward a half-inch of shooting space or, if the defense can be duped, toward a spin-and-drive to the basket. I was mesmerized by little things—a dip of the head, a twitch in the shoulder, a convincing set to the mouth—then a fall-away jumper, his slim body going up strong against the backdrop of the city streets. An incandescent moment with the sun around his head like a halo; then the ball rattling through the chains.

"One-o," said Harold. "I'm up."

He went left now, as if heading for the corner, then ignited in a curl toward the baseline. At eight feet he swiveled in a running hook that swirled twice around the iron before dropping.

"Two-o," he announced.

He banked in a jumper two steps left of the foul line. Then, going to his left again, a running floater. A reverse lay-up flipped back over his right shoulder. A hook shot from the right baseline.

"Six-o," he said. "Mine."

"Take it out," I answered.

In Seaside we'd played one-on-one a thousand times in the yard at the elementary school. There was sand on the court, and no net, and a sea wind to grow accustomed to. We'd sat against the wall of the school chewing gum and drinking soda pop when we were done. Harold was going to play for the Celtics one day; I was going to play for the Lakers.

A slashing lay-up from the left, protected. He missed, and I scored twice from the top. Seven to two, Harold.

In Seattle we found the sun fell pale and motionless and the chain net gave a satisfying *swush* when the ball passed through it. In Seattle we found an audience in passing cars and young couples decked out in tennis whites. In Seaside the throes of Pacific waves had forever been there, lulling me—the sound of my life passing. Now, in the city, there was no such sound, no vista from home of an endless ocean beyond which any possibility lay; in the city, I realized, there were millions of people, all like me: dreamers falling short of their absurd dreams.

Harold banked one in from thirty. He drove right, coiled through a three-sixty and released the basketball from the graceful fingertips of his left hand. Swish.

"Nine to two," he said. "My outs."

A jumper off the dribble drive, left. Down the middle, straight at my fear, the right knee in my chest, an exaggerated arc and off the board.

"Eleven-two," said Harold.

He missed from the top of the key. I struggled in low. A turnaround from five feet—in.

"Eleven-three," I said.

Once, in Seaside, we picked clean a cherry tree together. Harold, stains on his face, sat against its base spitting pits for distance while I watched him from a branch high above.

Two fall-aways. A scooping lay-up. Harold's breath, stinking of peanut butter. His elbows and most of all his tenacious rear end, bumping me out of position.

"Game point," announced Harold.

We'd gone smelt fishing together. Millions of them, spawning in the breakers, Harold and I yarding on our net in tandem while the Pacific smashed the sand around us.

He went right. I leaned into him; Harold leaned back, of course. And for a moment we were frozen that way, two islands of tension, the both of us seized up, intractable. He held the ball cradled between his hip and forearm, he ducked low, laying his shoulder against my chest. I could feel the spring coiling in him, and when he dipped away from me I followed forward brutally, going with his weight. Harold kept falling back, the ball looping over us and against the sky, far short of its mark, an airball, happily, and then that ligament in his knee buckled and snapped and his face darkened, a shadow formed in the pupil of his eye. I was standing over him and Harold was on the concrete, his knee braced in both hands, his face contorted in soundless pain. He seemed naked, exposed and utterly helpless while I stood over him, observing.

<center>~~~~~~~~~</center>

The evening astronauts first walked on the moon Harold was at the Children's Orthopedic Hospital. I went there too, and sat beside him with a transistor radio, and we heard Neil Armstrong tell the world that his was *one small step for man, one giant leap for mankind.* For some time we pondered the meaning of this; it seemed to Harold that Armstrong had left a word out. Didn't he mean *a* man had taken one small step toward peace for all of mankind? Yet my father, from the foot of the bed, insisted that either way Neil Armstrong was a phony—that the experience should have been beautiful, but that Armstrong was there so that one day, if necessary, we could knock the stuffing out of the Russians from the surface of the age-old moon.

We sat there in that hospital room and listened to men speak to us from the Sea of Tranquillity; Armstrong called it a "magnificent desolation"; then a broadcaster reported that a Russian probe, "bent on reconnaissance during the mission," was preparing, soon, to land in lunar soil. My father laughed at this, at which point my brother asked grimly for a dose of painkiller and I bolted through the door to find his nurse, thankful to have this convenient task to do for Harold just then.

<center>~~~~~~~~~</center>

My father never found a job in Seattle. For two weeks in August he labored at a flour mill on Harbor Island, a paid trainee who in the end would not be hired permanently. Each evening he came home with a film of flour dust against his skin and clothes, dressed in work whites and Converse tennis shoes, the smell of beer on his breath. Then it was over. My mother, using a yellow highlighting pen, marked those classified advertisements she felt in her heart he ought to give his attention to. She packed him a sack lunch and sent him off in the Bel Air to spend his days filling out forms. But to no avail, really. Whether it was self-willed, or the times, or both together, my father found no work in the city. Sometimes on fall evenings he would sit on the patio and smoke cigarette after cigarette in a shroud of silence, his head hung between his knees. This went on throughout that autumn until my mother's inheritance was depleted. Then my father took out a small business loan and bought up a parking lot in downtown Seattle, where he spent his days drinking coffee and reading magazines in a drafty and cold plywood hut.

My mother cleaned houses and the offices of dentists for many years in Seattle. It was what she knew how to do, and she was much in demand among the ladies of the North End, who found in her a methodical, reliable worker. With her hair tucked up under a scarf and not a speck of makeup to conceal her real face she looked downtrodden, weary. She died when she was forty-eight; the day before I had tried feeding her applesauce through a straw but my mother could not keep it down.

My brother stopped playing basketball. After his knee went he was through with sports, not because he had to be but because he wanted it that way. When I came home from practice he'd be wearing a sweater and looking at bugs through his microscope. On certain occasions he would look up at me as if mystified by what he beheld in my face; then his eye would travel to the lens again, leaving me out of its field of vision and focusing on something very small he never offered to share. It would stay there peering steadily down, insistently, patient, until I left in the direction of my own room—a solitary place.

*A*liens

~~~~~~

I met Dan Wyman in Auto Shop One, a course I took mainly to intrigue and offend certain acquaintances of mine at Roosevelt High School. These were kids I'd sat among for years in honors classes—kids who seemed to know where they were headed at fifteen, kids with clear reasons worked out inside for taking Business Law or Ancient History. *(How could they?* I used to ask myself. *How did they know with so much certainty what it was they would need?)* At fifteen I wore an overcoat from the Goodwill Store and shoulder-length, unkempt hair. That coat, as voluminous and awkward as a camping tent, a gray wool number with slack lapels and limp-threaded, large cuff buttons, made me a sort of celebrity, I thought. But I was wrong. I sensed without recognizing the special sort of loathing that here and there had been reserved for my appearance, but the more general unconcern for my existence in the world I couldn't perceive.

Strangely, I felt a widespread aversion to my character

most powerfully in the auto shop. The students there knew I was a Laurelhurst boy, a white-collar refugee merely trying on blue-collar life as a form of novelty or minor diversion. They were instinctively offended by my presence among them, as if I had made a game out of their lives or stepped across an invisible border into a nation where I didn't belong. Two or three times I was openly insulted when my obvious lack of experience with automobiles manifested itself to these guys. Then almost all thirty of them turned on me. "That's a fucking *spark plug,*" somebody would say. *"Counter*clockwise," somebody else would say. "Don't fuck around with those adjustments." "Don't be such a fucking idiot." "Don't touch *any*thing around here, all right, dipshit?"

Naturally I did my best to conceal my ineptitude. I talked a half-decent game, but sooner or later you had to take a tool in your hand in that course, and when I did there was no hope of sustaining the pretense. With each mistake, each embarrassing confusion, I retreated further into the silence of the tourist who knows he will never communicate. Even my hands seemed to become more tentative and unworkable in the face of the loathing I felt directed at me. I began to consider skipping, another strategy of mine, a flirtation with danger I knew would garner me even more inverse social status than my street wino's overcoat, since skipping involved putting your grades on the line and taking a chance, however insignificant, on being expelled or suspended. No *real* honors student would ever skip.

But how did I meet Dan Wyman? Fifteen lawn mower engines were clamped to workbenches around the auto shop and everybody, daily, paired up. The partners I had, as a matter of course, ignored me with a studied sullenness.

They picked up the tools and went to work. I stood there. Some universal agreement or unspoken policy prevented the unlucky greaser who drew me as a partner from extending the slightest measure of friendship. I became in that room an alien presence, an idea rather than a human being. But not with Wyman. He ignored me only until he needed a third hand, then asked straightforwardly for help. "Hold this down, please," he said softly, pointing with his cleft chin. "Hold this. Right here." So my hands began to work among his, that's all, and he exhibited no disgust for me. He even seemed ignorant of the sphere of animosity circumscribing my being, though in retrospect I don't think he really was. He didn't *care*. He had a knack for coaxing even the most recalcitrant engine to life, particularly when others asserted such a feat was impossible. The challenge of infinitely small physical problems arranged in a long and methodical series gave him a special pleasure. It dawned on me that, by the time he graduated, Wyman would be a paid mechanic. This was something he didn't seem to know yet. He took a completely innocent joy in his ability, viewing it as nothing special. His father, he said, was a flight mechanic in Texas; his brothers were also mechanics. His parents were divorced but when Wyman spoke of it his face did not indicate pain. He was muscular. His features were good. At the end of class each day he washed his strong hands carefully and combed his hair with water, parting it at the side. There was no graffiti scrawled on his notebook, as there was all over mine. He gave to the world the appearance of a neat, scrubbed, well-mannered boy, a budding Mr. Goodwrench, healthy and attractive but not in love with himself or fashion-conscious—the kind of boy who might be a marine someday, or a police officer, if he wanted to be. But he didn't. He'd cut himself off, I noticed, in a manner that precluded that kind of future. There was a distance between Wyman and everybody in that room, a studied distance, that he had placed there. He was always very quiet, very busy.

Once, while we were cleaning up our workbench and getting ready to leave, Wyman asked me a question.

"What's with the overcoat?"

"It was cheap," I said.

"They didn't have any that fit?" said Wyman.

"No, they didn't."

He was silent for a while. I could see that his brain was working on this problem. His face stayed even, but the movements with which he worked, putting tools away, sped up.

"You mostly get As?" he said.

"In some things. Yeah."

"Then why can't you spend a few bucks on a coat? One that fits?"

In his mind this made good sense. And in a way he was right. If I could get As I should be able to find a decent coat. Wyman wore a neat and trim Eddie Bauer jacket and, in courses like History and Algebra-Trig, received mostly low Bs and Cs.

"I don't know," I said. "I haven't gotten around to it, I guess."

"Oh," said Wyman.

"I hate going into stores."

"Same here," said Wyman.

"Besides, I don't mind this thing," I said, holding it by the lapels. "It's good enough. It does the job."

Wyman looked at me like he'd never seen my face before. "You look like a fucking bum," he said.

It was true. I knew it was true, but I just kept telling myself I was smarter than he was. "Hey, Wyman," I said. "I don't *care.*"

We put the tools away.

~~~~~~~~~~~~~

Wyman had a car, a blue Mustang. He was sixteen, mobile, good-looking. I got friendly with him, not exactly because of those things, but more because he didn't stop me. It was a strange sensation at first. We were *friends,* I realized. We began driving around a lot on weekend nights, looking—like most teenagers—for some ineffable great thing we assumed must be out there, some worthy thing to look for which remained unnamed but sought ceaselessly in the nighttime anyway. After a while it occurred to me we were looking for girls. *Obviously.* At that point I became self-conscious about it. We were looking for girls. It helped lend direction to the proceedings.

We drove around Seattle eating hamburgers from Herfy's. Wyman wrapped his in paper napkins and ate with exaggerated scrupulosity, occasionally stopping to wash up and collect himself. I wiped my hands on my overcoat while I waited, an all-purpose dress item, easy to care for. "You've got some hairs out of place," I would tell Wyman, or something like that, when he came back from the gas station rest room. Then he would go for his pocket comb and, nervously, lean into the rearview mirror.

"How is it now?"

"You fucking narcissist."

"Does it look okay?"

"They're all going to want you to come on their faces."

"Don't be *gross,* man."

"What's so fucking gross about that? Huh? What's gross about it, Wyman?"

"Shut up, okay?" said Wyman. "Stop playing with yourself."

"Eat mine. What's gross about it?"

But Wyman just shook his head and started up his Mustang, which always idled steadily and perfectly. "Sick, man," he said. "You are *sick.*"

I gradually became content with merely driving aimlessly, so it was a surprise to me when, one night in March, we actually located two girls. The prospect of this occurring had long since dissipated; it had become little more than an excuse to drive around together, fending off loneliness by sitting on the same seat, watching familiar streets swim past, spending the time with someone basically undemanding— though neither of us would have admitted to all this. In any event here were these girls with their thumbs out, down by the canal near Fremont. It was impossible to know whether or not they were beautiful—whether they were the girls I had imagined finding. They stood in the rain with big purses over their shoulders, dark and wet-looking at eleven-thirty, nothing but shadowy possibility. But Wyman wasn't slowing down.

"Hey," I said. "Pull over."

"Jesus," said Wyman. "Girls."

We had to go around the block once. Wyman wasn't ready and had to compose himself a little. "Girls," he said again. "Those were girls."

"Pull over this time," I reminded him.

When we veered in the second time they let their thumbs down. Wyman watched them critically through the windshield and so did I—two budding connoisseurs. "They look like a couple of *dogs,*" Wyman whispered. "Let's get the hell out of here."

But then they were piling into the backseat suddenly, reeking of cigarettes and cold Seattle rain. "A Mustang," said one of them. "Cool."

They were both dripping water from their hair and clothes—two soaked and pale girls in blue jeans.

"You like cars?" I said.

"Yeah."

"Dan here is Mr. Cars," I said. "I'm serious. Mr. Cars."

"Yeah?"

"No," Wyman called back over his shoulder. "Not really. Not at all."

I glared at him. Why would he take no advantage from this? His neutrality, which I interpreted as a brand of fear, irked me, and I nudged him. Wyman rolled his eyes in reply.

"You look sort of cold," he said into the rearview mirror. "I'll turn the heater on."

As we passed through the streetlights I looked them over under the guise of concern for their wet condition. The one who liked cars wore a red poplin jacket and soaked, bell-bottomed Navy jeans. Big-boned, freckled and colorless, she nevertheless had a kind of bovine attraction: somebody you might sink into, and from her white folds and pasty valleys never return. She sat there uncomfortably with her neck twisted to the left, wringing the water from her hair. I smiled at her, but my heart wasn't in it. She smiled back dreamily and put her hand across her mouth. Her fingers, too, were plump and pale; they worked with nothing akin to grace and watching them I felt the faint beginnings of disgust.

"I'm Joan," she said to me. "My stepbrother had a Mustang but he sold it."

"Really?"

"Yeah."

"What year?" I said.

"A sixty-seven."

"This one's a sixty-eight," I said.

"Sixty-nine," said Wyman.

"Yeah," I said. "A sixty-nine."

The other one, though more aloof, appeared more quietly inviting. Her silence suggested certain slim possibilities; her wetness suggested the kind of bathtub sex I'd gathered was adult fare from television. I liked her small head and exaggerated, damp mascara; I liked the idea of dominating her smallness and getting some secret fierceness, some agreeable, energetic acquiescence, in reply. She had red hair, a turned-up nose, brown lips.

"What's your name?" I said to her.

"Carla."

"Where do you go to school?"

"Where do *you* go, Buster?"

"Roosevelt," I said apologetically, since Roosevelt was the school of snobs and rich kids.

"It figures," she said, rolling her eyes. *"Roos*evelt. It figures."

She looked out the window disdainfully, rubbing her hands together, blowing into them.

"Is the heater on?" Joan called.

"Yes it is," answered Wyman.

"I'm *freezing,"* said Joan. *"Brrrr."*

"I'll turn up the fan," said Wyman.

"Wait a second," I said. "How exactly does it figure?"

"I'm sure," said Carla. "You can *tell.*"

She snapped open her bag, searched around with one hand and came up with a package of cigarettes. "Everything's soaked," she observed.

"*How* can you tell?" I said. "What is it, anyway?"

Carla rolled her eyes again. "It's the way they talk," she said crossly. "It's the weird stuff that comes out of their mouths."

Joan laughed, covered her face, then slapped Carla's shoulder with as much daintiness as she could muster.

"Lay off," she said. "They're giving us a ride, okay?"

"Wait a second," I said again. "How do they talk? Explain this."

"Like you," said Carla. "Got a light?"

Wyman pushed in his lighter. "Hold on," I said. "I talk like anybody talks."

"You talk like a Roosevelt guy."

"Oh, come on," Joan said. "Lay off, Carla."

Wyman pulled his lighter out, a glowing orange coil, and held it back over his shoulder. Carla leaned in and lit her cigarette.

"Thanks," she said.

"You're welcome," answered Wyman.

Somehow he was making more progress than I was by merely driving the car. The sensation of being so flagrantly rebuked was not so much familiar as it was inevitable, as though I had dreamed all this ahead of time. I decided to speak less, calm down, be courteous—as if I could change my character in the face of such distaste for it. I grew silent; we all did.

"Where am I taking you?" Wyman said after a while. "Is there an address or some place you'd like to go?"

"Home," said Carla. "Go out a hundred twenty-fifth."

"Okay," said Wyman. "Fine."

"Why don't we stop off for a bottle of wine?" I suggested. "How would you two like to drink some wine, maybe?"

But it was as though they had expected this from the beginning. Neither seemed impressed by the suggestion. Carla showed nothing in her face at all, but Joan began to wag a forefinger at me. "Naughty," she said. "Naughty, naughty." Then she produced from her bag three bottles of Ripple, the wine of choice among teenagers of those years. One of them was three-quarters gone.

"Automatic party," she said to me.

"Portable," I said. "Portable party."

"Whatever," Joan said. "I'm sure."

"Really," said Carla, still looking out the window.

It was the sort of conversation that seemed unavoidable that evening. These girls were strangers, slightly vulgar somehow, slightly cheap too, less fragrant than what I had always hoped for. I did not want to believe that the sort of girl I might end up with hitchhiked around from lonesome street corners carrying bottles of Ripple in her purse. I'd dropped a notch, on this rain-slicked evening, from the life my parents had held out to me. Wyman did not seem to feel this way. He seemed capable of carrying on with the business of driving and had fixed himself to the steering wheel with a sort of terminal rigidity. I could not count on him to aid me in easing the situation. Anything I said was an immediate blunder, a *faux pas,* which is a term no one in that car—except for me—could have possibly understood the meaning of. Still, I felt impelled to go on speaking somehow; this unfolding theater was my responsibility.

"What do you say we stop?" I pushed on. "Pull over, have a swig maybe. So Dan here doesn't have to drive."

"That's okay," answered Wyman.

Carla began to insert directions into the forward motion of things—left here, right there, go straight ahead—but without the tenor of polite apology one would expect in her situation. She never even removed the cigarette from between her lips; its fiery tip bobbed and glowed in the darkness as she spoke from around its filter. We had passed into a neighborhood without streetlights or sidewalks, a north Seattle neighborhood of weedy carports and faded ramblers within earshot of the interstate freeway.

"Right up here," said Carla. "On the left. Right here."

It was a house like all the rest of them, a low, flimsy-looking box. A boat trailer sat in front of it rusting; puddles lay where the lawn should have been.

"Is that your Barracuda?" asked Wyman.

"It's my brother's," she said. "He's in love with it."

"Cool car," I said. "Should we chug some of that wine now? I know I'm kind of thirsty."

Joan looked at Carla. "What do you think?" she said.

"Doesn't matter," answered Carla. "I don't care."

She yawned.

"Shut off the motor," I told Wyman.

He shut the motor off dutifully. I noticed the rain against the roof now, a frail rattle and roll. The Ripple went around in a counterclockwise fashion, tasting like watered-down Kool-Aid. I swallowed an enormous draught before passing it on to Wyman, who tilted the bottle in the most perfunctory manner possible, as though he drank from it only out of courtesy.

In the end we split that wine two ways. Carla merely wet her brown lips with it, but Joan drank with an eager greed, with desire, with misguided passion. It was as if she might find in those bottles of Ripple an answer to the most basic questions. I, too, drank as much as I could, shriveling in alcohol my self-disgust. As for Wyman, he remained uninterested in anything except keeping a courteous low profile. That wine went around at least nine or ten times without his swallowing more than a few tablespoons. It was as though he feared being poisoned.

"Aren't you worried about your parents?" he said finally, turning to look at Carla. "What if they see us out here?"

"They're asleep," Carla answered. "The lights are out."

"What if they wake up?"

"They won't."

"She's done this before," Joan threw in. "A lot of times, right, Carla?"

Carla didn't answer. She merely sat there, idling in neutral.

"Is everybody warm enough?" said Wyman.

"I'm not," Joan said. "But don't start the motor, please."

And it was then that I felt her hand in my hair, fingers toying with the locks at my neck, raveling them up, tugging. "Nice hair," she said to me. "I like it."

"You do?" I said.

"Yes."

I swiveled into the gaze she leveled me with, a gaze that meant *sex* in no uncertain terms, a gaze that meant nothing else'd turned out for her this night and that I was all that remained. It was that simple, but it stunned me anyway, and my thoughts swam beyond control now. She disgusted me, she was not what I wanted, and so, with the bottle of Ripple in my left hand, I climbed over into the backseat.

"Automatic party," I said.

"Really," said Joan, with her arm around my neck. "Right on. All right."

Wyman turned on the radio.

"Hey," said Joan. "You go up front, Carla. With that guy. Okay?"

"That's all right," said Wyman, peering through the rear-view mirror now. "I mean, unless you *want* to."

Carla looked out the window.

I was fifteen—basically an unattractive boy with pimples, in an overcoat. It was my first kiss: a girl named Joan. Nineteen-seventy-two. I recall ineluctably the surprisingly bad smell of it. Her mouth tasted terrible, like seaweed, like half-digested wine. *So this is it,* I kept thinking. Her tongue asserted its way into my mouth and then lay there like a piece of slimy rope. And I felt nothing, no desire for her: I couldn't feel her through the thickness of my overcoat, or breathe in the actuality of who she was. We touched only because we both hated ourselves; and so we were unable to feel each other. There was nothing either beautiful or easy about this. I began to feel I had ruined forever a moment that should have been fondly memorable. In adolescence it seems as if life might reveal itself only at the most poignant moments. But somehow these never arrive. Constantly consumed by small grievances of personality, we remain immune to their coming. We can't fathom anything finally, not love, not joy, not the truth of some other. Not the stirring of the spirit by the touch of the body. Nothing.

"I'm going," Carla said in the face of this scene. She opened her door two inches and peered out. "Call me," she said to Joan.

"Wait a sec," Joan said. "I'm coming."

She pushed me away from her, stared for a second into my eyes with some poor, misbegotten sense of her own grandeur in the moment—as if our brief meeting constituted high romantic tragedy—then bolted, dramatically, from the automobile.

"Thanks for the ride," Carla said to us.

I looked at her. If I had kissed her mouth would things have been different? Perhaps the fragrance I had dreamed lived there, just behind that disdainful expression. Perhaps you could melt down that penumbra of disdain—that tiredness about all the boys she had ever met—and reveal behind it whatever feeling adults had that made sex their favorite subject.

"You're welcome," answered Wyman. "Good night now."

When they were gone I tried to erase the taste of Joan from my mouth, but this was a noisy process. It seemed to me there was nothing to do with it, though; it wouldn't leave me or fade away. "She tasted like *shit,*" I said to Wyman. "She was *fucked.* Fucking *gross.*"

"Here," he said. "Wash your mouth out with this." And he held up a nearly full bottle of Ripple. "They forgot it," he said. "Jesus Christ."

I rinsed with the Ripple: but nothing could eradicate what Joan had done to me. Nothing. Not even Ripple wine.

~~~~~~~~~~~~~~~

Driving, Wyman lapsed into a rigid silence I was too self-absorbed to interpret. "You should have nailed that redhead," I kept saying to him for some reason. "She wanted you to, you know. She did."

"No way."

"Are you kidding, Wyman? Obviously. Fucking obvious. She wanted it."

But he didn't answer. He drove along with one hand on the steering wheel, the other busily grooming his immaculate hair.

"Maybe some Drano would get this smell out of my mouth," I said. "Joan," I said. "What a dog."

"German Shephcrd," said Wyman. "Spayed and neutered."

I laughed. So did Wyman. "The rain's slowing down," he said.

"Let's drink this Ripple."

"Let's go somewhere decent."

"Let's drink it at the Savoy. Up on the roof. We can climb the fire escape."

"Good idea," said Wyman. "Great."

He liked it for the same reasons I did: we would count on the night air, the volume of the gray sky, the misty view of the city from the roof of the hotel—we would count on all of it to wipe things clean somehow and make us undefiled once more. How were we to know such a thing was impossible? What is ever put behind you?

"Fucking *stinks,"* I said again, and rolled down my window. I turned my head and spit with the wind, but there was nothing satisfying about it.

"More Ripple," said Wyman. "Go on."

He was drinking himself now. He had a much finer genetic aptitude for it than I did. No doubt Wyman, wherever he is, drinks like a fish today. In any event at sixteen he could drink me under the table. And he liked to, generally speaking.

"That redhead would have spread," I said.

"No way," said Wyman.

"Bullshit."

"You're crazy."

"She wanted it, Wyman."

"That's crazy."

"How would you know?" I asked. "Huh? How would you?"

"You're full of shit," said Wyman.

It was a truth about myself I already recognized. But it hurt, coming from Wyman.

"Screw you," I said. "You're the one who's full of shit, you know. Why didn't you make a move on that girl? What's the matter with you?"

But he didn't answer. He only sucked down more wine and passed me the bottle without taking his eyes off the road.

"Drink up," he said. "Let's get drunk."

"I'm already drunk," I said.

"Get more drunk, then," insisted Wyman. "That's what I'm going to do."

I took a drink of wine, but it was true, I was drunk already, and anything I drank now just made me feel worse than I already felt, more wine-sick, more unhinged.

"Hey, Wyman," I said after a while. "How come your greaser buddies hate my guts?"

"Those guys aren't my buddies," Wyman said. "I don't even talk to them."

"Yeah, well, how come they hate me?"

"They don't hate you."

"Bullshit."

"They don't," said Wyman. "They don't even think about you. Nobody notices. Those grease monkeys don't think about anything."

"They won't talk to me," I pointed out.

Wyman looked over at me apologetically. "You want to know the truth?" he said. "Huh? Do you? All right it's that fucking *coat* of yours. You look like a fucking *clown* in that thing, okay? You make a fool of yourself."

"You think so?"

"Yeah."

"Then why do *you* hang around with me?"

"Hell if I know," said Wyman.

"You don't like my coat?"

"No. But I don't care. Wear the fucking thing if you think you have to."

"Fuck you," I said.

"Right," said Wyman.

We parked and climbed the fire escape to the roof of the Savoy Hotel: me in my overcoat, Wyman with a bottle of Ripple trapped between his underwear and the waistband of his pressed cordoroys. It was still raining just a little. We sat beneath some sort of overhang. From there the city spread out toward the salt water. There was no sense of action, of a life in the streets—Seattle seemed to exist as an addendum to the water, the sky and the listless rain, all more essential elements in the landscape.

"Nobody likes me," I pointed out after a while.

"Not true," answered Wyman firmly.

He put his arm around my neck then, something I'd never felt from anyone before—not friendship, not love, not sex, not solace even—just the sensation of something human finally, with no selfish motive attached.

"Forget about those guys, all right?" he said. "They're nothing but grease monkeys. They won't let a guy be different. Forget about them. They don't matter."

"It's not just them. It's everybody."

"Then forget it all," said Wyman. "Who cares? Forget it. Have another drink of wine."

"I can't forget it. It's not that easy."

"Take a drink of this."

I did.

It took Dan Wyman a half-hour to convince me. But in the end I threw my coat off that roof. "For you it's easy," Wyman said. "Toss the fucker. Go for it." So I stood at the edge of the city and tossed it. It floated at first, and then seemed to plummet, and at last it fell out of sight.

"Good move," said Wyman, clutching his bottle. "For you it's easy. It's just that simple." But I wasn't thinking of what Wyman might mean, or of why he couldn't shed *his* aloneness that easily: I was thinking, as usual, about myself instead, coat or not coat—of course I was.

This is a story with an epilogue, finally; there seems to be no other way to tell it. Wyman and I stopped being friends after a while, a thing that happened gradually, in a piecemeal fashion. There was no sudden falling off, just a gradual drift, currents dragging at us from opposite directions. It seemed to me the most normal thing in the world to move on emotionally in this manner. I wasn't hurt, and I don't suppose Wyman was either; we just went on becoming who we were, that's all.

When I was twenty-four I saw Wyman again in a bar in west Seattle. He was shooting pool with two other men, the three of them circling the table with their cues and leaning low into the smoky light there to take their shots with the utmost seriousness. It was not so much something in their appearance, or even in their manner, that suggested what I came to conclude from the scene: that Wyman was gay, a homosexual. It was rather their intimacy that suggested it, the way in which their pool game shut them off from the world and made them a society unto themselves, so that what the rest of the bar might think of them was a matter of complete insignificance. Wyman had grown a mustache. He seemed to be more of an adult than I was—he looked older, more knowledgeable about the rough-edged, seedy part of life than I would ever be. His face had gotten softer, his hair had receded, his body had thickened almost imperceptibly. But I noticed the details of his aging, of course, just as I've found I can't help but notice a lot of things about people. I had come there alone at midnight from my studio apartment in order to be in proximity to others for a while. I sat at the bar with my beer and watched Wyman. Once, as he moved past one of the men on his way toward the cue ball, he very gently placed his palm on his friend's buttock. The man smiled as he pondered the pool table. The third man leaned on his pool stick.

I didn't speak to him. I only watched. After a half-hour I wandered back to my apartment, where a novel I would never finish writing lay strewn across my desk. I looked for Wyman's picture in my high-school annual—searched for it with a curiosity I didn't know I possessed. *Daniel Richard Wyman* it said beneath his picture, a handsome boy in a white tuxedo suit, white teeth, combed hair. *Woodworking, Hunting, Automobiles.*

Wood Grouse

on a High Promontory

Overlooking Canada

~~~~~~

I went up there with my brother, Gary—up on the side of Goat Peak: a high promontory overlooking Canada.

That day we caught no fish at Wall Lake. They were there, watching what we did, but the weather was all wrong, too sultry, and the fish stayed down in the deep water.

That day Gary wouldn't talk about the war he'd only just come back from. "You don't want to know," he said to me. "Take my word for it, Bud." So after a while I didn't ask anymore. But I could see Gary had seen things I hadn't.

I don't know. I was fifteen. I spent a lot of time throwing rocks, I know that. Building stacks of rocks, backing off thirty yards, then throwing for as long as it took to knock the stacks of rocks apart.

We saw a flock of sheep, a sheepdog and a shepherd, up on the Wind Pass trail. "Aren't they beautiful?" said Gary. The shepherd was a silent Mexican on a horse, his dog a ragged mutt; the sheep flowed away from us in a slow white wave as we waded through them in the cloudless sunlight.

There were no trout for lunch but some cheese I'd kept in the streambed and a can of sardines and some dried pears. Then—later—we smeared ourselves with jungle juice, put our sunglasses on and took the compass and the Geological Survey map up on the side of Goat Peak.

Up there Gary spread the map out on a slab of rock, and laid the compass down and watched while it settled. "There's Canada," he said. "That's Eldorado Peak way over there and that's the Chilliwack Valley."

I looked up into a world of blue spruce that rolled on endlessly to a land I dreamed about. I didn't say a thing about this dream to my brother, though—about the mountains or about living off the land. It seemed the wrong dream to tell him about, now that he was back in America.

"This is the border," Gary said. "We're in Canada, Bud."

Driven into the scree up there we found the mounted iron border marker—number fifty-five, it read. We sat by it: a place to rest and watch the sun go down.

"Draft-dodger heaven," said Gary.

We kept crossing from country to country, back and forth, revelling in the freedom of not answering to anyone about it.

Eventually to the northwest there was no light other than a crescent of orange wavering on the horizon. The sky over our heads lit up, while the earth we sat on went cold in the last sweet twilight.

It was in this last light that we saw them—*hooters,* that was the name our father used—a covey of wood grouse dodging through a broken tumble of sharp gray talus rock.

"Look," Gary said. "There."

I picked up a stone about the size of a baseball and

watched them—imagining myself a hunter of wild animals.

"They're beautiful," Gary said. "Just look at them."

I let fly hard and in the gray light the covey scattered, a drilling of buzzing wings, birds tossing themselves down the mountainside, but one seemed to leap up so that for a moment it was painted like a shadow against the sky, the tips of its wings wide, a sound like *whoot whoot whoot whoot whoot to-whoot* aimed at the heavens, it did a half-roll in midflight and plummeted, describing an arc, headlong into the darkening scree.

"Jesus," Gary said. "What did you do that for?"

I had no good answer. I said, "I didn't think I was going to hit one, Gary."

We went down and stood by her where she was dying among the rocks. She was a large female—soot-colored tail feathers, some white hind shafts, a narrow, bluish band where her flanks narrowed. My stone had caught her flush in the breast. One wing had been crushed in her fall to earth.

"Jesus," Gary said. "Look what you did."

I didn't speak, though. What could I say? We stood there, the two of us, watching her.

"Jesus," Gary said again.

There was nothing left for her. The other birds were long gone. The one good wing only twitched along the rock. Her life flowed out of her, into the scree, back into the earth it had come from.

"I'm going to finish this pain," Gary said. "God forgive me."

There were tears in his eyes I hadn't figured on.

He put his boot on the dying bird's head—the sole over one alert, clear eye—and ground it suddenly into the rock while the wings gave a last frenzied shudder. They fluttered out to their full span spasmodically in the moment just before she died.

"That's it," Gary said, not ashamed of his crying—just crying now while he spoke to me. "That's all it is. That's all there is to it, Bud."

We went down the mountain and around the canyon head to Wall Lake. No trout were feeding there; not a sound except the croaking of the marsh frogs.

After we had eaten the pinto beans with chili powder and white rice for supper we sat by the propane stove for a while.

"How has it been?" Gary asked. "What have you been up to?"

I told him about not making the basketball team, the fight I'd had with Mike Kizinski, other things that didn't really matter.

"I like hearing all this," Gary said. "Tell me some more, Bud."

But I didn't. I was young and didn't know any better. So instead I asked him about the thing on my mind: "Did you kill anyone in Vietnam?" I said.

"Did I kill anyone in Vietnam?" said Gary.

"Did you?"

"Did I kill anyone in Vietnam," said Gary. "Did I kill anyone in Vietnam."

And again he began to cry silently, in a way I hadn't figured on at all.

"I'm sorry," I said. "Really."

But he went on crying. He cried with no shame. He cried

in a way I didn't think was possible. He didn't rub his eyes or try to stop it. He just cried.

~~~~~~~~~~~~

Later we took down our sleeping bags from where they'd been airing over the branch of an arctic pine, and laid them out on the flat ground we'd cleared the night before. The two of us lay buried in our bags, only our faces showing, the drawstrings pulled around our heads so that the spilling of the snowmelt over the pebbles in the streambed was like a muted roar, a streaming music beginning and ending in our ears. We lay there side by side staring up at the stars, and talked about how unfathomable was the phrase *light years,* the possibility of life on Saturn's seventh moon, the years that would have to pass before NASA put a man on Mars. We talked about a theory Gary read about in a book—that time and space didn't really exist, that everything was in reality something else we didn't know about.

After a while we gave up on the useless things and watched for the points of light that were satellites among the forever-fixed stars. We watched them hurtling slowly to the horizon, gravity tugging them always toward the earth so that they moved in a relentless straight line out of vision. Gary said that, if need be, a satellite could take a close-up photograph of us in our sleeping bags, as soon as the sky became light enough.

"But it doesn't matter," he said. "It's beautiful up here. I'm glad we came. I'm glad we're here."

I heard him, minutes later, moving toward sleep, and I began to feel alone among all those mountains. And then I couldn't fall asleep that night; I felt ashamed of myself. But later on I found that Gary was awake too, and then we passed the dark hours talking.

"Two insomniacs," he said after a while. "Crazy, Bud. Insane."

"At least we've got someone to talk to," I said.

"At least we've got that," said Gary.

*P*iranhas

~~~~~~

*T*he door of Paul's bedroom opened one evening and his parents and their dinner guests came in.

"Paul's room," his mother announced. "And Paul."

"And is this connected to the intercom system?"

"Certainly it is. The whole house is."

"So you can call him for dinner. How convenient."

"If there were such a thing as dinner," said Paul's mother. "If dinner existed, yes."

She laughed, airily, at her own words.

The guests fanned out, looking at things with calm detachment, absorbed by the walls, the floor. Paul, his hands in his lap, sat on the edge of his bed and watched them silently.

"He has his own television," someone pointed out.

"He has his own television, yes," said Paul's mother.

"Strictly regulated," added his father. "The homework has to get done right before the television comes on at night."

The guests eyed Paul with curiosity now. He thought he

knew what they were thinking, though—was he the sort of boy who had trouble at school? Was his homework a family problem?

"What grade are you in, Paul?" somebody asked.

"Seventh," his mother said. "We started him early."

"Look at this," one of the guests insisted. "The dial on this intercom's turned all the way down. How can he hear anything?"

"He can't," said Paul's mother. "We never use that, really. It's just there."

"I've always thought that about intercoms. You can't justify the expense."

"Oh, come on," answered Paul's mother. "Let me tell you something. It came in handy when Paul was a baby. We could monitor his crying from upstairs."

"Well how much is an intercom system? Let's hear some figures on this."

"I don't remember," Paul's mother answered.

"It came with the house," said Paul's father.

"Well, what good is it if you don't use it?" said the guest. "It's just a lot of useless wires running through the walls."

"That's it," said Paul's mother. "Useless wires."

For some reason everybody laughed at these words. Then, as if by some unspoken agreement, it was time for the house tour to move on.

"Hey, Paul," somebody said. "You're one lucky guy living in a place like this. And I bet you don't even appreciate it."

Once again, everybody stared at Paul. They stood together in a group near the doorway, drinks in their hands, bored.

"He's the silent type," explained Paul's mother. "Say goodbye to everybody, Paul."

"Good-bye," Paul said. "See you."

They went out. He could hear them in the hall. "Let me show you my new hot tub," his mother was saying. "It's *wonderful.*"

Walking home in the rain on Monday afternoon, Paul slipped into the pet shop on Sixty-fifth Street.

"Wet out," the man at the counter said in greeting. "You know what I'm saying? *Wet.*"

The man wore a square mustache and black plastic glasses. He stood at the cash register with a pencil behind his ear eating popcorn from a brown paper bag, and looking, to Paul, a little sinister for some reason. His shop had the vaguely menacing aura of a laboratory set up in a cave. Four rows of aquariums stretched away into the darkness. Only they were lit—nothing else. The fish hovered as if in a dream, secure in their lit glass houses. The place smelled of jungle; vapor fogged all its windows. In another room caged birds sang.

"Wow," Paul said. "It's neat in here."

"Look around," the man advised. "Go ahead. Dry off. Put your books down and look some."

"Okay," Paul said. "Thanks."

He wandered between the rows, peering into each tank with his hands on his knees, feeling immense suddenly. The man had hung a placard over each aquarium: PARADISEFISH —FROM TAIWAN; CHOCOLATE GOURAMI—THE MALAY PENINSULA; BANDED CLIMBING PERCH—THE ZAIRE BASIN. The imprisoned fish appeared to lead effortless and aimless lives. They hung suspended in corners, one eye to the glass, or tipped themselves toward the membrane of the surface. Some swam diligently, but most seemed to understand there was no point to that. They went wherever the water took them as it bubbled up from the filters.

Paul watched them for some time. He decided—though he had no words for it—that they lived in a private and trivial universe, subject to currents of thought so removed from their lives that their identities as individual fish had been submerged. Perhaps they had known all the miseries of capture; perhaps in transport from some exotic home the unassailable loneliness of the world had been revealed to them. Now they swung about in watery cages, forgetting or remembering, uncertain if what occurred in the course of their hours constituted an actual existence. Paul, with a conscious exertion of the imagination, thought of them as they might have been in their other lives—free, inhabiting a warm and boundless ocean, darting joyfully, their hearts light, feeding, in conquest, at liberty to live. He thought of them as cultivating a preordained singularity, nurtured by forces that were rightfully in effect, according to the universe's grand plan.

When he looked up the man at the counter was watching him suspiciously. He still stood behind his cash register stuffing his mouth with popcorn.

"You're interested," he said to Paul. "I can tell."

Paul nodded.

"Start small," the man advised. "Ten gallons, max. Decide if you like it, then move up gradual. You've got all kinds of time."

"I already know I like it," Paul said.

The man crammed more popcorn between his lips. "Oh, yeah?" he said. "How can you tell?"

"I just can," Paul said. "I'm like that."

"Well," said the man. "Fine then. If you know yourself that well, *fine.*"

~~~~~~~~~~~~~

Paul came upstairs at six-thirty. His parents were in their living room now—he'd heard them turn the lock fifteen minutes before, he'd given them time to get settled. The television was on: news. His father sat in the wing chair with his feet across an ottoman, listening through headphones to the CD player, pieces of the mail scattered on the floor beside him. His mother—her feet pulled up beneath her on the sofa—leafed through a mail-order catalog.

"Hello," Paul said to them. "You're home."

His father pried off the headphones. "Hello," he said. "Did you use the VCR after school, Paul? I noticed someone left the power on."

"No," Paul said. "I didn't."

"You're wasting electricity," his mother said.

"I didn't use it," Paul repeated.

They stopped talking in order to watch a television advertisement. A car rose up from the surface of the road and flew off into the glitter of deep space. Then it returned, a woman got into it. A man in jeans, leaning jauntily against the side of a barn, watched her flash by. She went around a corner, got out in front of a nightclub. A man played a saxophone beside a water fountain, sweating. The woman was driving again, her lavender fingernails trailing across the upholstery. A man sitting in front of a gas station, the sun setting in the mountains behind him, scratched his head as she blew past.

"Boring," announced Paul's mother, and turned a page in her mail-order catalog.

Paul wandered into the kitchen. For a while he opened cabinets, looking at things—noodles, canned olives, bottled salad dressing. His father came in and went to the refrigerator, pulled out a beer, snapped it open and drank leaning against the counter.

"We can microwave," he said, loosening his tie. "Sound okay to you, Paul?"

Paul nodded.

His father opened the freezer door. "Beef stroganoff," he announced. "Halibut in cream sauce, pasta marinara, shrimp gumbo—what'll it be?"

"Beef stroganoff," Paul said.

"I'm for halibut," said his father.

His father opened the microwave oven. "Can I get an aquarium?" Paul asked.

"What?"

"I want to buy an aquarium," said Paul.

"An aquarium?" said his father. "What for?"

"I just want one, that's all. Can I?"

"I don't know," said his father. "You'd better ask your mother, Paul."

They went into the living room together.

"An aquarium," said his mother. "Where do you want to keep it?"

"In my room," Paul answered. "Please?"

"Is it messy?"

"No."

"Who's going to clean it when it needs to be cleaned?"

"I will. I promise, Mom."

"I don't know," said his mother.

She turned the pages of her catalog.

"It's not like a dog or a cat," said his father. "Personally, I'm for it, Kim."

"Why do you want fish?" said his mother.

"I don't know," answered Paul.

"All you can do is *look* at them," said his mother.

"I know that," said Paul.

"How much money are we talking about?"

"I don't know," Paul told her. "I could use my Christmas money, though."

His mother tossed her catalog on the coffee table. She stood, tossed her bangs from her eyes, brushed a wrinkle from the front of her skirt and—stretching toward the ceiling, only her toes still touching the carpet, her hands balled into fists above her head—she yawned.

"No," she said. "You leave your Christmas money in the bank, all right? *I'll* pay for the aquarium."

"*I* want to pay for it," Paul said.

"You can't," said his mother. "*I* want to."

~~~~~~~~~~~~~~~~

Ken, a friend from school, a boy who wore a ski parka and who put gel in his blond hair, came to look at the new aquarium one afternoon.

"Weird," he said. "That one with the thing on his nose."

"That's an elephant fish," Paul said.

"What's with this one?"

"That's a severum. He got his tail chewed. That guy there—the Jack Dempsey?—he does it. He's *rude.*"

"Cool," said Ken. "Do they fight?"

"No."

"You ever see a Siamese fighting fish?"

"No."

"I saw it on television," Ken explained. "It's so cool. They kill each other. You throw them in a tank together and watch them *brawl.*"

"Really?"

"People bet on them, I think in China."

"Really?"

"It's so cool," Ken said.

"You ever see two cats wrestle?" Paul asked. "It's so cool. They—"

"They're *screwing,*" Ken said. "That's different."

Paul fell silent.

"What're the ones with the stripes?" Ken asked.

"Those are tiger barbs."

"They're kind of small."

"Yeah. Sort of."

"Maybe the Jack Dempsey fish could eat those guys. How come they're not all chewed up?"

"They're fast," Paul said. "They get away."

"Well, what about the blue ones? They don't look so fast."

"I don't know," Paul said. "Those are gouramis. The Dempsey leaves those guys alone."

"What's this?" Ken said, tapping the glass of the tank. "This one? Right over here?"

"That's a red-tailed shark."

"Cool," said Ken. "What does he eat?"

"They all eat the same stuff," Paul explained. "This."

He held up the can of Tetramin. "It's like leaves and stuff," he said to Ken.

"Maybe you ought to throw in some *meat,*" Ken advised. "So they can get bigger—they're pretty dinky looking."

"They don't get big," explained Paul. "You want them to get big, you put them in a bigger tank."

"You ever see that movie?" Ken asked. "This girl goes down to South America with her dad. He's a scientist or something. She takes her clothes off to go swimming and these *piranhas* eat her. It's so *cool,*" he added.

"I saw that," Paul said. "Gross."

"It grossed my friend out," Ken said. "*I* didn't get grossed out, though. You remember when that scientist guy gets it?"

"*That* was gross. That was *really* gross."

"Yeah," said Ken. "You want to go to the arcade with me?"

"I can't," said Paul. "My parents won't let me."

"Neither will mine," Ken said.

At night, every light turned off but the one in the aquarium, Paul watched his fish from the safety of his comforter. Their eternal passivity struck him as offensive: their hearts should boil over, they ought to dash their brains against the glass. But they were only fish and so they hovered, ghosts of themselves, unrealized souls. They could not concoct a plan of escape or rail against their condition. There was no identifiable question for them to ask, and anyway their world was warm and luminous and food appeared in it at regular intervals. What would it mean to be a fish and did they hear him when he spoke out loud? And when his face was pressed against the glass was he there for them, or was he nothing? And what did they make of the formality of their world, its lines and corners, its cramped geometry? Were their brains pitched to the proper degree of uselessness, in order that contented lives might be lived in such conditions as these?

Even a fish must experience captivity as some agonizing, ceaseless form of suffering. There together, living out entire lives in maddening, langorous comfort, they must gently become unhinged in the head; either that or die. And so they circled, or hung in the void, or sulked, inert, above the gravel. They hated and ignored one another endlessly, and when the light in their home went off at night they slept with thankfulness that their world had been erased until morning returned it to them. And this they lived through—Paul decided—with thoughts commensurate to their station in the order of being, as it had been explained to him at school recently: these fish, because they were not anything but fish, were condemned to only the faintest understanding of matters, perhaps to none at all; no one knew.

Paul, on the other hand, would grow older and understand. In fact he was beginning to understand already; he was twelve.

"Piranhas?" the man at the pet shop said, cleaning his glasses on his shirttail. "Piranhas are vicious, all right? They'll mess up your other fish in no time."

"I saw this movie," said Paul. "They eat you."

"Only if you go in the water," said the man with a wink. "Come here and have a look."

They went down between the rows of aquariums. They came to a tank with rust-red gravel, algae mottling its sides. The man stopped by it, grave-faced. Then, strangely, he began to hum the theme from *Jaws*.

"Piranhas," he announced. "There."

Paul looked in. A dozen fish traveled in a group restlessly, silver, deep-bodied, blunt-headed animals, no bigger than fifty-cent pieces.

"A lot of people buy them," the man explained. "Basically you've got two choices. You start a separate piranha tank— nothing but, just piranhas, that's all. Or you throw them in with your other fish and raise them vegetarian-like. Never let them get the taste of meat, pretty soon they're docile like the rest. You have to figure there's an instinct, though. They start in chewing on someone's fins or tail, pull them quick— they're trouble."

"Pull them?" Paul said. "Where?"

"You can flush them down your toilet," the man explained. "They won't live up around here—too cold."

He leaned down and tapped on the aquarium glass. The piranhas flashed away for a half-second, a wave of movement, undulant, then fell back into their silent weaving.

"Check this out," the man said. "Their teeth are like little triangles. That's real teeth—dentine and enamel. Little razors, two rows of them."

Paul leaned down with his hands on his knees. The man put his index finger against the aquarium glass and pointed, absurdly, at the moving fish. "Teeth," he said. "Vicious little suckers."

"How much are they?" Paul asked.

The man looked at him. He took off his glasses, then looked again. He kept blinking.

"You're interested," he said. "Well, let me tell you something. Piranhas are a *habit,* okay? You get dedicated or you flush them. There's no in between. You feed them meat they get expensive, you don't they get boring—just another fish. You understand what I'm saying?"

"I think I do," Paul answered.

"Good," said the man. "Fine."

They stood there for a moment looking in at the piranhas. "Well," said the man. "I'll leave you alone here so you can mull it over. You let me know what you decide."

"I'll take eight," Paul told him. "How much are they?"

"Eight?" said the man. "You'll need another tank for that, you know. Eight? That's a lot to start with."

"I like them," Paul said. "They're interesting."

———————————

Ken stood looking into the new aquarium, situated next to the first one. "All right," he said, bending down to look more closely. "Just like the ones in the *movie.*"

Paul sat down on the edge of his bed. The piranhas spoke for themselves.

"What do you feed them?" Ken said.

"Whatever," Paul said. "You know."

"Like what?"

"Like tuna fish, mainly. Other stuff."

"Insects?"

"No."

"Like what then?"

"Tadpoles," Paul said. "I got them at school. They're in that jar over there."

"Cool," Ken said. "I want to see."

"It's not that big a deal," Paul said.

Ken picked up the jar of tadpoles. "Can I dump some in?" he asked. "Please?"

"Go ahead," Paul answered.

They watched together while the piranhas ate. It was quite leisurely, finally. No mad frenzy. They maneuvered, the tadpoles wriggled to no avail. Calm feeding.

"See?" Paul said. "I think it's from living in the tank or something. They don't go crazy like in the movie."

"The movie was better," Ken agreed.

"I read about them in the encyclopedia," Paul said. "They live in this river somewhere. A cow comes in, they turn it into a skeleton. They swim around in big groups, hunting. They find another fish, they eat it. People, too, sometimes. Natives washing their clothes and stuff."

"No kidding?" Ken said. "For real?"

Paul didn't answer. He lay back on his bed.

"Hey," said Ken. "Why don't you feed them something big, maybe? Maybe they'll go crazy eating it."

"Like what?" Paul said.

"Like a goldfish or something. You know, a fish. Throw one in and see what happens."

"What for?" said Paul.

"You know," said Ken. "So they can *eat* it."

"I thought about that," Paul said.

~~~~~~~~~~~~~~~

They were evil, he saw at night, blind in their purpose, communally devoted to the shedding of blood. Watching them Paul understood the liberation that came with such a shared lust: the piranhas—it was their instinct—had stepped across an invisible boundary, relinquishing their identities in exchange for the assurances of cooperation with ten thousand others. He could not even feel, rightfully, that he owned them really; they defied proprietorship; their allegiance was to one another. They were a single organism, each a part of something larger than the self. And none was alone—they brought what made them whole with them into captivity, then clung to it in defiance of reality. As with the other fish, on nights before, he imagined them engaged in their former lives—undulating with thousands of other fish of like kind, the scent of meat propelling them all across the river currents, the warm, safe riot of the hunting attack, the rapture of blood. He dreamed that in some other life he had known this feeling, too: safe among masses of those like himself, engaged to the pit of his being in a world of purpose, passion, sustenance, action, and finding within its context that impossible thing, love, boundless acceptance, a rightful place in things.

One night, having watched them late, he went out onto the deck of the house. He wanted, if possible, to see the stars or moon—whatever was up there: anything. But instead his parents were in their hot tub kissing violently, and his father's hands were on his mother's breasts; they surged up out of the water together and his father's pale, starved rump emerged and his mother's brown heels were pinned against his father's hamstrings. He saw that theirs was an angry passion that would not be satisfied; that love was like everything else in their lives; he felt this, watching them—the violence of their dissatisfaction with everything.

His mother kissed his father's neck, his hairy shoulder, his earlobe, and then her cheek was against his and she was staring into Paul's eyes. "Get out of here," she snarled. "Honestly, Paul." Paul's father swiveled and stared at him, too. "Paul," he said. "Jesus Christ."

They fell apart into the water. His mother took a glass of wine from the edge of the tub. His father laughed into the darkness.

"What's so funny?" Paul said.

"How about giving us a little privacy?" said his mother.

"Sorry," Paul said. "It was an accident."

"Go to bed," said his father. "It's late, Paul. Okay?"

He laughed again. Paul's mother took another sip from her wine. She moved over onto his father's lap.

"Are you getting the message?" she said to Paul. "Leave already, okay?"

~~~~~~~~~~~~~~

He went in and fed a blue gourami to the piranhas. They worked on it together, methodically. They nipped out a piece here, a piece there, tail and fins first, then along the flanks, finally at the back of the head. The gourami turned belly up before long. Later Paul fished out the skeleton.

He fed them the red-tailed shark the next night. It was no contest—they ate her with astonishing speed. The pair of severums went in together. The tiger barbs had to be tired out. The Dempsey fought, then died and was devoured. The elephant fish was the last to go. They accosted her from all sides; the blood was substantial. She floundered and the piranhas stripped flesh from her flanks until everything was gone but the bone.

Later the housecleaning woman, Molly, came into Paul's room and saw the empty tank with its hood left open, the water circulating through the filters, the pump humming along, the thermostat light glowing—but no fish, nothing, just water. She mentioned this curiosity to Paul's mother.

"They all died," Paul explained to her. "That's what."

"Well, did you take care of them?" said his mother. "Did you feed them?"

"I took care of them," Paul said. "Sure I fed them."

"Well, then what happened?"

"I don't know."

"Well, what did you do with them?"

"I flushed them down the toilet."

"Oh, God," said his mother. "Honestly."

His father came into his room that night. He sat on Paul's desk and put his feet on Paul's chair. He looked at the fish tanks and sighed.

"I see you split up the piranhas," he said. "How come, Paul? What's the deal?"

"They'll get bigger," said Paul. "This gives them more room."

"Don't you think they're big enough already?" asked his father. "They're getting *huge.*"

"No way," said Paul.

They were silent for a moment. The filter pumps hummed. The television was on upstairs.

"You have to get rid of these piranhas," said his father. "And I'm not asking you. I'm telling you."

"How come?" said Paul.

"Because they're *strange,*" said his father. "That's why."

"What's strange about them?"

"They're just strange. They're strange, Paul, you can't have them in your room like this. They—"

"Come on," Paul said. "Please?"

His father shook his head. "You have to get rid of them," he said. "That's all there is to it."

"No way," Paul said. "Come on, Dad."

His father leaned around the doorjamb. "Kim!" he yelled. "Come down here!"

"Come on, Dad," Paul said one more time.

His mother came in. She looked at each of them, one at a time. "Now what?" she said. "What is it?"

"Confrontation," said his father. "You're better at it, Kim."

"He's twelve," said Paul's mother. "You can handle it."

"I'm keeping my piranhas," Paul said.

"No you're not," said his mother.

"Yes I am," said Paul. "They're not hurting anything."

"Listen," said his mother. "The piranhas are going. Is that understood? Just remember who paid for all those fish in the first place. I paid, I'm going to make the decisions."

"I wanted to use my Christmas money," Paul said. "All right, fine—I'll get rid of them. Then I'll buy some more with my *own* money."

"No you won't," said his mother. "This is it with the tropical fish, Paul. You'll have to find a more appropriate hobby."

She went over and pulled the plug on the electric pumps. The bubbles stopped running through the filters.

"Leave it unplugged," she said. "I'm serious."

"Maybe Paul can take them back to the pet store," said his father. "Wouldn't that be better?"

"Paul can resolve this however he sees fit," said his mother. "Just as long as he gets them out of here."

There was silence then. Paul curled up on his bed. He pulled the pillow over his head, tucked his knees against his chest and swore under his breath at both of them.

"Did you hear me, Paul?" said his mother.

"Get out of here," Paul yelled. "I mean it."

Paul, in the morning, put the piranhas in the hot tub. They died immediately; he left them there.

He told Ken about it. They skipped school in memory of the dead fish. "My parents suck," Paul said.

"So do mine," answered Ken.

"I hate them," said Paul. "Big time."

"Same here," Ken said.

They walked across the golf course together. They cut across a sand trap to the ninth green. It had begun to rain; no one was golfing.

"I just want to *kill* them," Paul said.

"I want to kill mine, too."

"What's the best way?"

"Poison their food."

"Cut them up with an ax while they're asleep."

"Cut the brake line in the car."

"Shoot them in the back while they're taking a shower."

"We can trade," Ken said. "Like on television. You kill mine while I kill yours."

"I know," said Paul. "With a *chainsaw.*"

They sat on a bench. It was raining harder now. Cars went by on the road. Paul imagined how it might be to kill his parents. The thought caused him only minor remorse, because he felt certain they deserved it, somehow.

"Let's head over to the arcade," Ken said. "Maybe someone else'll be there."

Paul got up and pulled the collar of his coat against his neck, but the rain was inside of it now.

"All right," he said. "Let's."

Three Hunters

I came down through Echo Canyon, wading and rock hopping in Echo Creek, and the Game Department man who had spoken of silver trout was a liar by now and the creek screamed as it fell toward the Columbia. It was too hot, the water rode too low between its banks—even the black flies had finished hatching. The fish—all of them—had gone somewhere else. They were not in the creek anymore. They had disappeared from the upper lakes. They had gone to a place no one could walk into. I dreamed of that country while I followed the watercourse down between cracked rock walls and the leaves far above shook in a hot wind. Nothing else touched me; I forgot to watch anything else. In my dream I had enough to do, filling my creel full of silver trout. They were big ones but not much for eating and they fought much harder than the real ones ever did. They never got away from you either.

I was sixteen. There was nothing else on my mind.

When I had the dust path under my feet again my feet were surprised. The dust made my nostrils tighten up. A few pine needles that had gone rust-red in the late heat floated past me. I hiked through a grove of birches where the path snaked to avoid falling into Lost Lake and the wind brought the dust up around the backs of my waders. The birches were getting short on leaves.

For September, late September, it felt hotter than I could remember, but everyone talked about Septembers I didn't know about that might have been hotter—even my mother, who seemed to have no memories of anything and never spoke about the past to us or anyone else. Places, people, days, months, whole years had hardened inside of her until there were no good juices left, until there were only the bitter ones. She was a fierce woman, keen, her eyes like the points of arrows, her hair as black as her eyes. The town whispered about her, about her still mouth, her silent eyes, her past, but she showed no interest in words anymore. Her luck had been bad. She had nobody left to blame. My father had been smart enough to disappear before she killed him slowly, though nobody I knew looked at it in just that way. My mother didn't, for one; she insisted it had all been his fault, if she touched on it at all, that he had been too hard to be a husband. But I never listened when she spoke about him.

What did I care, though—about the town, my mother, or even the Game Department man who had lied to me through the mustache that crawled over his filmy teeth? I was here. One of my dream fish jumped out of the white sky. I watched the drops of water spiral away from his silver flanks, the sun so strong on them it hurt my eyes, then line spun away from me and then the path reappeared, dust and curling leaves, under my feet where it belonged.

A crow rasped somewhere in the woods as I came down over the cliffline, speaking to no one, to the wind. I followed a game trail now, I was no longer in the path; loose stones my waders kicked up bounded down to the shore of Lost Lake, disappearing in thick clots of thornbush as they flew along. I stopped and rifled a couple of big chunk-rocks into the water, inspecting the splashes they made closely, but none of them could satisfy me. They were only splashes— nothing more. The water settled back over them as though nothing had ever happened and the lake ignored me completely.

I slapped across Lost Creek, waders flying up to kick the creek-bed stones, and made my way into camp through the old fir forest that had never been cut because of the cliffs.

"Are you hungry yet?" Lane said to me.

He was sitting in the packed dirt next to the firepit, stripped down to his underpants, dealing solitaire with an air of great seriousness about him, as if solitaire held something no one else could ever know about, as if solitaire were some kind of ceremony. His face looked bruised and bloody, but the only thing he'd wrestled with had been the blackberries on the far side of the lake.

"Roy?" he said.

I frowned at him, at his underwear, at his purple teeth.

"I'm hungry," he said into his cards.

Lane was twelve. He had no memories of our father, who had left us—I thought—to save his own skin. He was thin, too; his long shoulder blades plowed the air behind him like a pair of dorsal fins. A lean kind of tension gave stiffness to his limbs, as though he were ready to jump into the woods at any moment. An alertness ran through him, but he was too young to contain it. It overflowed at his eyes.

I had one memory that was vivid, though: my father striding up a broad stretch of the Little Nelson River in his chest waders, canvas short-vest and spread-brim Stetson while I watched him discreetly from my perch on a boulder below the cutbank. He was like a giant barreling steadily upstream, fly rod in hand and smiling stiffly as he crashed toward me, and then with a hand that was powerful and certain he scooped me up beneath his underarm and we traveled together through the spring runoff, lunging toward the bend in the watercourse.

I rested my fishing rod against a pine bough. There were new scratches on the reel spool cover from the rock walls in the canyon. I loosened the straps on my daypack and set it down beneath a tent line. Everything in camp looked familiar and smelled of fir smoke, even Lane.

"Who's winning?" I said.

He brushed a mosquito from his forearm with the queen of spades.

"Nobody wins when you play this, stupid," he said.

"Then why are you playing?"

"I don't know."

I sat down. I fought my waders until they had no choice but to let go of me, then dumped a half-quart of water out of each.

Lying back beside the stones of the firepit I felt sleep coming, and my dream of the country where the fish had gone slipped through a crevice and returned. It was a silent bit of country first of all; nobody fished there but me. When the big silvers jackknifed past the surface of the water their gill covers shone and the parr marks along both flanks rippled and when you brought one alongside, played out and puffing, the flat serene eye of the fish spoke to you softly.

There were no mosquitoes in the dream. There were no other fishermen. There was nothing you had come out of and nothing you were going into, either: no home and no future. Winter never came in the dream—the fish ate always and the water stayed temperate. The fish were not plants from the State Hatchery, either; the Game Department man had nothing to do with them; they were all wild, natives: they went with the dream.

I had one; I had my forefinger hooked under the gill cover of a sleek silver male and I was looking down through the perfect fragile young eye that told nothing, that did not even seem concerned with death or exhaustion because those things were not real—

"Somebody's coming," Lane said, and threw his cards in the dirt.

We sat there, Lane in his underpants, me in my wet socks, and watched the three hunters work their way across the flat. Lane sprang up and got his jeans on, then sat down again on my side of the firepit.

"Zip your pants up," I told him.

They carried big game guns, bolt-action rifles that were impossible not to stare at, neither in cases nor lashed to their loads but instead out and at hand. One of them had a tumpline across his forehead, but the others were bent under the weight of their packs. You could not make out what the stink was that traveled with them—sweat, grease, musk, tobacco, stale whiskey, sour leather—but it was powerful enough, and it arrived before they did. They were downwind hunters, like all men.

"Hello!" I said when they were in our clearing, standing up in my wet socks to meet them.

"Hello." The one with the tumpline looked at Lane. "What

happened to your face?" he asked.

"Nothing."

"He's been eating blackberries," I said.

"Blackberries?" the hunter with the tumpline said to me. "Blackberries? Are you kidding me?" He turned to the other two, who were grinning from under their heavy loads.

"Did he say something about blackberries?" one of them said.

"Maybe we didn't hear him just right," suggested the other.

"Let's try this again," said Tumpline. "Did you say something about *blackberries?*"

"I guess so." My jaw felt tight. "I don't know."

Tumpline let go a sigh of disgust.

"Maybe we better just forget about it," he said, shaking his head at me sadly.

He twisted himself free of his pack and laid his gun down. The others followed suit. One of them wore camouflage pants; his gut hung down over the lip of the waistband like a cow's udder. I looked for his eyes, but they were three-quarters hidden under pasty lids. Pimples and sores festered across his bare back; thorn cuts—mottled streaks—crisscrossed his forearms; dark blotches stood up where the mosquitoes had nipped him. He looked uncomfortable, as though his body composed some private form of torture.

The second one sprawled out over his pack with his rifle next to him and stared silently at the tops of the trees. Crisp blond hair rose out of his head like the bristles of a stiff brush, greased into a whipped tuft at a widow's peak that grew slightly off center. He looked to me like a gigantic choirboy—someone who had grown absurdly large but had changed in no other way since the age of twelve. A scatter of blond peach fuzz clung to his chin; his cheeks were frosted with nearly invisible cottony whorls: otherwise he looked twelve and no older. He went shirtless beneath his combat vest and his muscles—the chest swelled too far, the neck cords thick and squat—seemed unreal and dispropor- tionate, like sacs of air beneath a layer of plastic skin.

Tumpline, though, was the bulkiest of the three. He had a lumpy, stubborn appearance—everything about him was huge but unsolid. His sideburns, a deep black-orange color, grew long and pointed toward the corners of his mouth. Sweat glued his hair down over one ear; the grains of his beard stood up like a mat of dark seed grass attached to his face. His lips, blistered and meaty, reminded me of night crawlers. He had gleeful, large-socketed eyes.

It occurred to me that, for some reason, big men always stuck together. They like it that way. They understand each other. Nobody else knows how they feel.

The fat one picked up my rod. He pushed up the bail arm, tightened the drag down, and began to practice his casting moves under the trees.

"You got that all wrong, Frank," Tumpline said. "You're supposed to use that near water."

Frank mumbled something to himself.

"Ain't that right, Big Guy?" Tumpline asked me.

"Sure."

"Sure," Tumpline agreed. He picked up a few of the play- ing cards and held them out for the blond one to see.

"Cardsharks," he said.

"Cardsharks," said the blond one, still staring off into the treetops.

Tumpline dropped the cards, one by one, in the dirt. "Ever been to Reno, Big Guy?"

"No."

"What about him?"

Lane shook his head at the forest floor.

"Never been to Reno," Tumpline said—to himself, or to no one. He picked at a molar and looked over our camp for the first time.

"Where's your catch at, Big Guy?"

"I didn't catch any."

Tumpline's plump, raw lips parted. "Big Guy," he complained. "Big Guy, come on now. Do I look like an asshole?"

"No."

"Sure he does," the blond one threw in. "He looks like an asshole."

His eyes never moved from whatever he had noticed in the tops of the trees.

"Now wait a minute." Tumpline scratched at the root of one sideburn with an index finger. "Just a minute here. I don't believe this. You hiked the fuck up here—am I right?—I mean you hiked *all the way the fuck up here*"—he stood and flopped his arms at the sky; his mouth moved but no words came—" . . . it's all too incredible, Big Guy," he finally said. "I mean it's just too fucking-A *incredible.*"

The blond one stood up now and unzipped his pants calmly. "I told you he was an asshole," he said, and took a leak with his back to us.

"You." Tumpline was pacing now. "You—*Little* Big Guy. I want you to tell me the truth. I want you to think hard for a minute here and tell me what the truth is."

"Okay!" Lane answered.

"Good." Tumpline saluted for some reason, snapping it off his forehead so that the salute ended two feet in front of his eyes. "Very good. Excellent. I can see you want to cooperate. It makes me feel good when I see that."

He double-stepped in a sort of dance around the firepit and crashed down on the ground next to Lane.

"Little Big Guy," he began, "you are my friend. Don't ever forget that. I don't want you ever to forget that."

"Okay," Lane said.

"Okay?" asked Tumpline. "Okay. Now listen. It makes me feel good to sit here next to you. It makes me feel I can trust you—do you know what I mean? Don't answer that. Just sit there. Don't even *think* about moving. Just answer my question. I need you to answer me. I need the *truth,* for once. I need to know where the fish are up here. I need your knowledge, everything you know, Little Big Guy. Don't hide it from me. Don't be selfish, good buddy, *share* it. Be cool. Tell me what I need to know."

"I don't know anything, though," Lane whimpered.

Tumpline slapped his forehead. "I'm disappointed in you," he said gravely. "I'm very, very disappointed in you."

He rose and stepped away from us like a man who's been bitten by a snake, then turned suddenly beneath the silent firs.

"Leave me alone," he cursed us now, his eyes bubbling and strange. "All of you. I mean it. I have to think this all through . . . what I'm going to do and everything. There are big, *big* decisions to be made. You haven't heard the last of me, you assholes."

"Shut up," the blond one said coolly.

Tumpline stumbled away toward the lake. When I turned to check on Lane he stared back wildly, his face shimmering with addled blood.

"Everything's okay," I told him.

The blond one unzipped a side pocket on his pack and

brought out a tin of Copenhagen. He tamped a chew in against his gums, then leaned back again with his hands behind the base of his neck.

"Don't mind Mickey," he told us. "His brain don't work right anymore."

"All right," I said.

"I know the dude," he said through his chew. "He got his mind blown—can't think straight anymore—but he ain't dangerous. Sometimes you just have to put up with this shit from him, that's all."

"Sure," I said.

"It's a waiting game is all," the blond hunter went on. "When he gets done fucking around here he's gonna be ready to *hunt*. . . ."

He spit, a five-foot riser that cleared the ends of his boots and clapped the dirt in front of him like a shard of buckshot. "What did you say your name was?"

"Roy."

"You didn't catch no fish?"

"No, sir."

"Maybe you ain't much of a fisherman."

"I'm not," I said.

"Shit," the blond hunter said. "It ain't got nothing to do with you."

He picked up his gun now, and rubbed circles with the ball of his thumb across the oiled stock. He seemed to have forgotten us suddenly. The fat one, swinging my rod between the trees, appeared lost in a world of his own conjuring. He cocked his wrist, casting laterally, his belly rolling like a wave beneath his T-shirt, the rod tip jumping and then stiffening at the peak of its arc. Occasionally he would stop and casually massage and knead his breasts, or touch his belly knowingly, or paste his hair against his forehead, running his hand over his cheeks as if to gauge the extent of their fatness. He ignored everything—us, the forest, the blond hunter lolling on his pack and spitting chew—absorbed in his body and my rod.

I stripped off my wet socks and draped them over the biggest of the stones that ringed the firepit. Then, barefoot, I tidied up the camp. I stowed my daypack inside the tent and zipped the mosquito netting over it. I closed the tent flaps. I stuffed some sardine tins and soup packages and the bag full of flapjack mix inside my trailpack and lashed it shut. When everything seemed in good order I unzipped one of my side pockets and slipped my fillet knife, buckled inside its leather sheath, behind the elastic band of my underpants.

"Stay cool," the blond hunter said when I turned around again. "I don't give a shit what your camp looks like."

I nodded. The fillet knife punched against my hipbone. The blond hunter cradled his gun in his arms and stared up through the branches of the firs. I considered him, his gun, my knife, the trees, then swiveled once more around on my bare heels and unlashed my trailpack. I searched through my things for a dry pair of socks, and when it seemed right I dropped the fillet knife into a side pocket.

Tumpline came weaving into camp between the tree trunks. When he reached his pack he picked up the rifle that lay across it and pointed it at me.

"I didn't want to have to do this," he said evenly.

"Then don't," the blond one answered him. "Put that thing down."

"Who do you think you're talking to, Private Fields?"

"Didn't I tell you about his brains?" Fields asked me.

Tumpline clicked off his safety, then pulled back the action on the rifle. His eyes seemed to have retracted even deeper into their sockets, like things at the backs of two caves. "You see this, asshole? This is a Mauser. It carries a magnum cartridge. One hundred-eighty-grain bullets. It could tear a hole where your face is, Big Guy."

The fat one had come back to the real world. He was staring at me from almost directly behind Tumpline, still clinging to my rod.

My throat wasn't working. Tumpline's index finger lay against the trigger; the Mauser was leveled at my chest. I had to stare at Tumpline, into his eyes—it seemed as if that was all that kept him from shooting me. Finally, I dropped my dry pair of socks. I locked my knees—my bladder felt ready to give up its load—and held my hands up over my head because I didn't know what else to do. The balled socks rolled over the dirt like a baseball.

"Don't shoot!" I said. I sounded to myself like someone who had just had their tonsils removed.

Lane was crying now, without making any noises except ones I could hear, the way he did at night sometimes for no immediate reason. I wanted to say something, anything, it was up to me to tell him what he needed to hear, but my throat had seized up and the blue barrel of the Mauser with Tumpline behind it held me frozen in place while the fat hunter gaped and the blond one, Fields, chewed.

"It ain't loaded," Fields said calmly. "Nobody hikes with a loaded rifle."

"How do you know?" Tumpline swung the Mauser around.

"Pick up your socks," Fields said.

I dropped my hands. The Mauser swung back—I flinched, but nothing happened. Finally, Tumpline broke into a grin and set the butt of his rifle on the ground. *Nobody hikes with a loaded rifle,* I told myself. I picked up the balled socks and sat down by the firepit, but my fingers couldn't figure out how to put the socks on. It didn't matter—nothing mattered. Lane cried—it was something he did with his face, soundless, undetectable to the three hunters—and Tumpline balanced his Mauser against one of the tent lines, barrel up.

"What a fucked-up waste of time," Fields muttered to the sky.

Tumpline only pulled at his bottom lip. "Is that yours?" he said to the fat hunter.

The fat one looked at my rod as if he had never seen it before. "Me?" he asked.

"Is it yours?"

"No."

"Then put it down."

He did, sheepishly. Then he stood with his hands at the small of his back.

Tumpline swung his pack up now. "Let's get out of here," he said. "There's nothing for us here, Private Fields." He pulled the leather tumpline over the top of his head and anchored it just above his eyes, then picked up the Mauser.

"There is nothing here," he repeated, as if it meant something to anyone but himself.

They drank from their canteens, cinched in their waistbands, took in the slack in their shoulder straps. Fields ejected his chew. The fat one spread bug juice over his cheeks and neck and now his raw skin glistened in the heat. They took their guns up.

"Be cool," Fields said as they tramped past the firepit.

"Yeah," the fat one echoed. "Be cool."

Tumpline never looked at us. "You're going to be dead," he whispered to the ground.

Sticks and dry cones popped under their boots—stones skidded from the game trail above Lost Lake and gravel sprayed down through the thickets below the cliffs. One of them spoke, not words but a rumble, fading as it vibrated through the trees. Finally they went up over the cliffline, through the gap and into the dust path, and we stopped listening for them.

"Roy?" Lane whispered.

The forest was more silent than it had been, the trees more firmly rooted. Everything seemed solidly entrenched in the blue light of evening over Lost Lake.

"Let's go home," Lane said, trembling.

"What for?" I said.

"They might come back."

"They're not coming back."

"They might. Those guys are crazy."

"Get your shoes on," I said. "And bring in some firewood."

That night the weather finally broke. I woke three times to hear the west wind rippling our rain fly; the fourth time I lay back with my hands behind my head and rain popped against the nylon. Lane, burrowed down inside his sleeping bag, breathed in short gasps through his nose, sputtering and wheezing through his dreams. Gradually the sound of the rain hardened into a kind of shattering and the rest of the night sounds disappeared. I gave up listening for the three hunters; they wouldn't move in the rain; they wouldn't move anyway, I knew they had forgotten us, but I couldn't forget them: Tumpline's dark retracted eyes looking out from behind the barrel of his Mauser. I kicked my feet at his image but there was no solace in it. The rain gathered in a crescendo.

Asleep I waded downriver, fishing the untainted place again. Water broke around the backs of my knees as I fed line to the edge of the current. The only sound echoed from the river itself, a quiet thrashing. Then the line went taut, the rod bent double, the reel shrieked and ratcheted and a silver trout large as a seagoing salmon broke from the clear surface, dazzling in the sunlight.

She ran downstream, and the reel spool paid out line. I hauled back. The trout leapt fiercely, impaled deep on the slender hook, and from fifty yards I saw the blood foaming in her mouth.

The sky darkened as I brought her alongside. I slipped my finger under one gill cover. When I pulled her from the river, two feet long and fat, meaty, her eggs in their transparent mucus began to slip out of her—hundreds of them dripping down into the river and streaming away.

I didn't want to keep her for some reason. Her great eye shimmered, distorted, miserable. I worked at the hook as delicately as I could, but I ripped her apart anyway and the dark blood streamed from the corner of her mouth. I began to shake and the rain came. When I set her down on the water again she sank gently, wobbling, and in a great curve foundered and came belly up, riding away forever on the river current.

~~~~~~~~~~~~~~~~~~

We walked down Main Street in our packs in the rain, and when we passed the Game Department office I mentally cursed Neil Reuthens, the Game Department man. Neil Reuthens didn't count now—I knew that. *The bastards,* I kept saying to myself, because the three hunters had come back to town with me when I had tried to leave them at Lost Lake; *the bastards, the bastards,* and the phrase fell evenly inside the rhythm of my walk as I stamped home through the patter of the rain.

It was Sunday. A State Patrol cruiser, muddy at the rear, sat in front of the Elk Lounge. A few cars were angle-parked in front of the Shop-Rite, and one at the Premier Realty office, but otherwise there was only the rain. Things looked the way they always looked—silent, bored and unchanging. Nothing seemed to move except the puddles, and they only popped when the rain hit them, settling and stirring beneath a thin, gray sky.

The bastards, the bastards, the sons of bitches . . . my lips moved in this cadence but it didn't help, nothing helped: I couldn't get that vision of Tumpline's dark retracted eyes out of my mind.

Main Street, wide and desolate, merged into Highway 26 before us, beyond the town limit, at the bridge over the Little Nelson River. We turned into Kiksiu Street with the backs of our necks to the sky—dead box elder leaves ground into bleak mush by the rain swamped the gutters— and cut through the thistle and high weeds to our house. Our mother's dark blue Pinto sat in the yard, its rear end rusted orange, the hood held down with chicken wire. Dick Gleaton's cats had pushed the lids off the garbage cans again.

"Don't tell her about yesterday," I told Lane—but I didn't know I wouldn't tell her myself. "She doesn't have to know about it, okay?"

"I wasn't going to say anything, peckerwood," Lane said.

"Who's the peckerwood?"

"You are."

But she wasn't home, predictably, and the heat was on too high; rain drummed against the windowpanes and the screen door clattered in the wind. An odor of rotting fruit rose from the garbage bin next to the sink, a sweet sickly humid smell that permeated everything. Lane switched the television on immediately and sat down in front of it. Grown men were bowling on the screen, eying the pins heroically over the tops of their balls and following their casts through with absolute mechanical precision.

I went into the bathroom, to the mirror, to myself. *The bastards,* I said silently, staring at my face, *the bastards, the bastards,* but when I came out nothing had changed. Lane had fallen asleep before the television.

I went into the kitchen and took down a tall can of chili and a bag of rolls, but the garbage smell was too strong and I took the bin outside into the rain. I went around to the front and fixed the screen door so it wouldn't batter the siding all night and then, for some reason, I pitched a stone at my mother's Pinto, denting the side wall by the back fender.

"Bastards!" I said out loud, and the rain swallowed the empty word quickly. Kiksiu Street, empty itself except for the rain and the box elder trees, looked dismal and small beneath the sharp wall of green firs that buttressed the mountains to the north.

In the kitchen again I poured the chili with its ring of orange fat into a pan and lit the old gas stove. Standing in the refrigerator door I took a long pull from a carton of milk patiently going sour on the upper shelf. The milk tasted slightly rancid. A wilted-looking pineapple had rolled over onto its side down below. I drank off part of the syrup from a large can of Freestone peaches and as I

stood there with the metal fruit can in my hand the compartment light suddenly flickered out, throwing the back of each shelf into darkness. I reached in, sliding one of the freestone halves into my mouth at the same time, and broke the bulb with my fist, and then, as I drank off more of the peach syrup, my mother slipped in through the back door, quietly.

"Back from the wilds," she said, and sat down, wet and flush-faced, and threw her purse easily on the kitchen table. Unconsciously, by force of habit, she plugged the coffee pot in.

"Back from the wilds," I said.

"Any luck?"

I shook my head grimly. "Where have you been?" I asked her.

My mother turned and folded her coat across the back of the chair with careful deliberation. Then she looked me in the eye, evenly.

"What's wrong?" she said.

I ran a spoon through the chili. "Nothing," my voice said. "There were these hunters up by Lost Lake. Three of them. They gave us a bad time."

"Who were they?"

"I don't know."

"Did they hurt you?"

"Not really," I said. "One of them pointed a rifle at me—he was a crazy bastard."

"Jesus Christ," my mother answered, and all of her fierceness began to display itself now; her black eyes went steel and her mouth narrowed. "Did you know your daddy did that to me, Roy? Aimed his rifle at me? Did you know that?"

"No, ma'am," I said, and I looked back down into the pan of chili.

"He did," my mother's hard voice said. "He aimed his rifle at me. Drunk and brave and home from the hills. Right here in this kitchen."

I lowered the flame and went over to the table, where my mother picked bitterly at a thumbnail, and I sat in the chair across from her.

"Mom?" I said.

She looked up, but her eyes gave nothing. They were like shields.

"I can't stop thinking about them," I told her. "I've been thinking and thinking about them and I can't stop."

My mother glared down at her thumbnail again and made a show of complete concentration.

"There are evil men in the world," she said. "Do you think you can change that, Roy?"

American Elm

I grew up in Wilkes, Rhode Island, where the light in early
winter seems to roll off the backs of the clouds and ignite
along the waters of ponds and millstreams, and the cold rot
smell of the barren forests comes ghostly out of the tough
earth, and the gold air and sky have a muted volume of both
space and spirit broken only by the reach of church spires,
soft-white and giant against the slow maple hills. My father,
gaunt-cheeked and patient of hand, was proprietor of the
Wilkes Bakery, a dark windowfront on Main Street with a
faint, tarnished sleighbell tied inside its door and a deep
odor of hot glaze and butter gentled by the calm warmth of
its ovens and the soft silver of its racks and pans. Rooted in
his quiet kitchen my father worked like someone in a dream,
wasting no part of himself on hurry, imparting the meditation of his work to the familiar recipes so that what came
forth from his hand carried with it, in its cast on the lips and
tongue, a residue of his inner peace. At dawn, in the first

pale light, my sister Ruthie and I chipped and scrubbed the long baking sheets and yellow mixing bowls. My mother stood behind the cash register, hair bound to the top of her head with dark pins, and bagged Persian buns and fried doughboys for the early millworkers who were our neighbors, the people of Wilkes. We lived over the bakery in rooms of aged and intricate woodwork, and the warm air of the ovens floated up through the floorboards, and there were lace doilies shaped like snowflakes on all the tabletops, and an oak rocker by a tall window through which that spacious light swarmed in early winter, a tender, fragile light that no longer seems to be in the world I live in today, though perhaps it is here and I no longer know how to look for it or see it, twenty years and thousands of miles from Wilkes as it once was.

In the summer of that year I write of now I made bales in the hayfields all up and down the township, and in the fall, my first of no school, I felled black oaks and sugar maples along the backsides of pastures, making firewood in the sharp sun while twisting leaves blew past the long arc of my splitting maul. In November, when north winds rattled away the last leaves and sent them skittering across the plowed-down fields, I found a new job in the Burrillville Sanatorium. Here, from eight until five, I washed the hands and feet and faces of the old of our township, and fed them cream of wheat and beet soup from small spoons pressed against their lips; I carted dinner trays and spray-cleaned bedpans and, bundling them up against the frost and cold, wheeled the old ones out to the riffled shore of Harrow's Pond where they would look out over the water and trees and sky in ponderous silence while I watched for shiners or for the ripple of bass in the marsh and lily pads.

It was eight miles from Wilkes and the bakery if you cut from the main route and, following the millstream, trudged your way over the Quampus Lake Road to Harrow's Pond and the border with Massachusetts, where the Burrillville Sanatorium lay shadowed in a thicket of pines. It was three and a half miles if, lighting out true north from directly behind the Wilkes Baptist Church, you took to the woods and pastures and, keeping your bearing accurate, twisted among the etched and lifeless trees and hopped the strewn rock walls dividing nothing any longer in the gray pallid light of the forest until, traversing a gradual knoll overgrown with furrowed slippery elms, you walked out onto the frosty, ordered grounds beyond the conclave of high brick buildings that housed the sanatorium.

Following quietly the mist of my breath I hiked with my lunch bucket each morning through the thickets and fields, the flaps of my duck hunter's cap turned over my ears and my compass inside my left glove. I scared up pheasants—a wicked, stick-crackling, wing-filled explosion out of deep brush that stopped your heart, and then a drilling, a buzz, as the fiery bird spluttered its way through trees to a deeper hollow. Without stopping for a moment I threw stones to crack the ice in ravines I crossed, and slipped under fences to walk the empty hayfields and silent apple orchards, swinging my black bucket as I went. At the sanatorium I hung my mackinaw over a hook, tucked my lunch in a corner, and ran warm water over my fingers before going up to the rooms and wards where the old people waited in the soft, waxen light that filtered through the pines beyond their windows. Afterward, in deep dusk—the woods too black to walk in—I rode back to town with Sam Mathers in his chopped and blocked blue-waxed Ford, slapped up the

stairs behind the darkened bakery to eat supper with my
family while the stars blinked on and spread themselves out
across the valley and the white North Star, already steadfast
over the steeple of the Wilkes Baptist Church, pointed the
way back again to the Burrillville Sanatorium and the waters
of black Harrow's Pond.

One morning in late November a faint snow came flailing
lightly, dusting the hard fields with a coat like powdered
sugar but, unable to pierce the stark branches of the silent
trees, leaving the woods dry and bare. At just under two
miles in my journey I crunched over a hayfield and crossed
the old Vaughan Road, a narrow paved lane that cut along
the banks of lonely ponds, intersecting the township from
northeast to southwest, writhing in among the silver maples
and leaning oaks of the third-growth forest. Thinking on it
now—snow twirling, gray sunlight expansive over frosted
pastures—I must have seen him first from a distance of a
hundred yards, moving laterally through my frame of vision
along the Vaughan Road and against the backdrop of still,
frozen trees. My memory—my memory I say—is of stepping up onto the fixity of pavement and eyeing covertly a
bent and weathered little man in steel spectacles who
clutched fiercely the tip of his pipestem between teeth yellow as pine pitch; who wore a duck hunter's cap like my own
with the bill turned up and the flaps turned down and the
buckle strapped and denting a chin like a red potato; who
seemed to be cursing, muttering and nattering at the ground
as he jounced over the Vaughan Road, looking up now and
then out of eyes hard as granite, glaring more or less, keeping friends and enemies at a distance from them—halting
the swing of my lunch bucket from thirty yards—a man who,
when he held his head up, the strain ran through his neck,

the Adam's apple rose like a strawberry in the crease of the throat, the temples—veined inkwell blue, protuberant—leapt out at me as the head fell forward; and then afterward the back of him, the stride game but broken, the old back heaving under a red-and-black-checked mackinaw and the spine itself knobbed and torqued, inhumanly twisted, a history of sweat mapped out in joints and cartilage (while the weight shunted from side to side as he thrust out his hard black Hitchcocks, the gloved hands felt the air, the pant legs gathered and ungathered smoothly over the spindly thighs, the whole of him barreled and bobbled—a slow barreling, a slow bobbling—over the chipped, worn pavement)—and finally the dark, delicate lines of the woods once more, seven-eighteen by my Grandfather Harper's tarnished pocket watch, the tiny weight of my compass lodged beneath my glove, wavering toward north in its dark place and the old early sojourner—a glance through the clean, acute trees—nothing but wisps of smoky breath, a *pock* over the surface of the Vaughan Road.

A sharp clash of sticks stirred one evening in early December—the second week it must have been: red, blue and muffled yellow lights laced the fretwork of the bakery—and in the night the wind slammed beneath a shimmering half-moon, the lightning cracked wide the blackness, the thunder rocketed off the rooftops of Wilkes and the high branches of the trees swirled madly beyond the gloss of street lamps that flared at the corners of our building on Main Street. In the morning—wind blowing now like a thin, cold sheet, the backside of the storm hurrying past to catch up with the turmoil at the heart of it—I tramped out toward the sanatorium past blowdown snags and cracked green windfalls that had barberchaired and crashed to the hard earth in the night, past split branches trashed up against mounds of underbrush, mangled and twisted and the brush swept south by the cutting edge of the north storm. I flung myself over the rail fence at the hay pasture on the Vaughan Road and clipped on toward work and the old ones with the wind flitting low now, skimming around my knees and ankles, and the sky overhead shot through with hard-riding clouds. I kept my head cocked downward; brush snapped behind me in a swale as the wind blustered through it, sounding like secrets the woods told themselves.

And there he was again: there he was again like some apparition—like a presence in some tale my Grandfather Harper might have conjured forth on an evening in winter long ago—in the guarded light and fleeting wind of morning tottering toward me over the fissured pavement, one brittle, almost transparent, liver-spotted hand anchored to the bowl of his cold pipe, and the buckle of his duck hunter's cap dangling down past his chin, tapping against his Adam's apple as he foundered over the road, keeling as he went like an ancient ship in a shiproad. "Hold up there, boy!" he shouted, at ease with commands, like a general of troops—the side of his mouth twisting open and the words tumbling out into the light and wind. "Hold up there! Whoa!"

I held my ground, the fingers of one hand curled under the handle of my lunch bucket, the palm of the other cupped to my compass, balanced that way and watching him come at me with whatever strange thing it was he wanted driving him on. For his part, he drew himself up when there were two good yards of road left between us—the regional courtesy, that; a metaphor for the kept-distance between human beings in our township—and yanking his pipe free so as to aim the cracked tip of its stem at the bridge of my nose, narrowed his eyes behind the thick glass of his spectacles and said, "What in the *hell* do you think you're doing, boy? What in the *hell*, boy? You answer me that!"

I took a step sideways, backing off imperceptibly, groping but at a loss for an answer that was not as ridiculous or abstract as the old man's question. In the precarious silence, like a hammer, the pipe fell downward and then flashed again, and the old man's face seized up in anger.

"What's your fambly name, boy?"

"Harper, sir."

He poked his pipe between his teeth and mulled. "Bak'ry Harpers? Is that what you be?"

"Yes, sir."

"Granddaddy Ezra Harper? Hay farmer up here?"

"Yes, sir. Only he passed on a few years back."

He slid a tattered tobacco pouch from the pocket of his mackinaw. And he began to knock his pipe against his hipbone now, holding the bowl up to the light every so often and peering up into it critically, blinking and grumbling in the bottom of his throat. "How many times you figure you crossed my field there—" pointing with the round of his chin toward the hay pasture, his pipe held trembling in the air "—in the last month or so, young Harper—speak up!"

But I couldn't. "I don't know," I stammered faintly, and the pipe came down once more and lodged, finally, in the tobacco pouch.

"Well, I do," the old man said, digging absent-mindedly, bits of dark makings blowing out behind him over the road. "Twenty-three times—now don't deny it—I been countin'

ever last one. 'Crost land 'tain't yourn, too, boy. Mine instead. You understand me?"

"Yes, sir."

"Yes, sir, hell," he boomed. "You kin 'yes, sir' me all
day, boy—'twon't come to naught," and he pulled his lips
tight while the wind rose up and blustered across his
cheeks and spectacles. "Now listen here: I'm liable to run
you in, Harper; don't care two nickels for trespassers—no,
sir, I don't. Don't care for 'em a 'tall." He slipped his
loaded pipe between his lips, thumb pressed over the
bowl like a cork, and let it totter up and down while he
spoke. "Your granddaddy don't care for 'em, neither," he
threw in. "Not that I know of, leastwise. Surprised he don't
warn you off from the likes of trespassin'. Don't make
much sense. You sure you're a Harper?"

"I'm one," I said. "Same name as him, sir. Ezra."

The old man shook his head, dismayed.

"Well, I guess it don't matter now," he sighed. "You and
me as best get on to the subject of reparations, boy—you
know 'bout reparations? Says just what it means. You done
some damage and now you're agoin' to *repair* it. Dispel that
notion I've taken to run you right along in. Fair is fair, see.
I figure a full day's worth of chores might 'bout do it far as
I'm concerned. 'Taint much for ever step you tramped
'crost my field, now is it, Harper?" He dug a wooden kitchen
match from the breast pocket of his mackinaw, struck it—
one trembling swipe—across the seat of his pants, then
frowned while it flared and snuffed out in the wind, cursed
and tossed it and struck another—the same scenario precisely this second time, only the muttered curses newly
sonorous, increasing in breadth and acidity—*blamed wind!
friggin' blast from hell! be damned!*—while the lit match

died between his blackened fingers. With the opposite hand he plucked his cold pipe free again, smacked his lips soundly and said, " 'Taint no perticular directions to give— fust place up the road here quarter-mile back—pineboard farmhouse, covered garage out front—leave you your own choice of days, boy, but Satidays is most always best—*early* Satidays don't you know; you got anything to say for yourself, Harper?"

But again, I didn't. "Be prompt then, boy, Satiday morning"—the old man said it like a reprimand. And I agreed to it all by not disagreeing and slipped off through the motionless black oaks of the forest, heading for the Burrillville Sanatorium.

There came to me flickerings of my grandfather as I went, though, disturbed as I was by the old man in the Vaughan Road—they come to me now: shreds of things that perhaps add up to nothing more than nostalgia and self-deception— of searching on our knees, he and I, for the chuck key of a drill on the floor of his toolshed—the one trailing image I have left of his face, which was open and gentle and gaunt like my father's as his huge magnificent hands roamed among the spiraled bits rolling over the packed dirt floor; of stalking his wide back through the pine woods beyond his haybarn *(This here was an apple orchard,* he'd pointed out, drawing himself up in the soughing breeze of that spring day—*growed over now with all this here white pine. Warn't no good anyway . . . too sandy . . . apples had a tinny taste to 'em—pie apples, mostly. Right off down there? You see where I'm a pointin'? That ol' bog? That was a pond oncet, Ezra. Can you make it out? We dug it ourselves, set by it summers . . . by God, by God . . . this right here was all apples oncet, though. . . .)* In his cellar were tools no one makes any more—an adze, a froe, a peeler spud turned by hand—the cellar itself he'd dug after the house was up, by moonlight and the odor of wick oil and without missing church while my father hauled barrows of earth and stone and root to dump in the woods. In his spare time he'd been a rabble-rouser, so they said, Ezra Harper, at the mills and town meetings; he'd shot himself in the knee once with a squirrel gun; he'd flung a man through the window of a tavern one night. He'd told stories—about a man named Flinch and his water wand in a time of drought, about lovers who stole his apples one autumn when Truman was on the stump, about a night's drunk, a clay jug, a battle in the woods—all with a tuck of deception at the corner of his mouth as he spun his sternly told yarns. And as I tracked along toward work and the old ones that morning I saw him as clear as clear water one ragged autumn in a deep place in the woods, miles and miles back in a place of frozen mud where leaves crunched into powder beneath your footstep—up knobs, through swales, amid bogs with their stale effluvium of death where weedy cottonwoods grow in silence—and he'd stopped, Grandfather Harper, somewhere in the perpetual forest, stamping his boots speculatively and pointing a finger at a line of curious stones. "I buried your grandma there," he'd said, matter-of-fact, plain speaking, and the two of us had waited in a silence as difficult as any I have ever known, stood there before the row of real stones watching until he scratched his head and stamped his boots again and led on through the dark forest to a place where spring water rose from a cleft in the roots of a chestnut.

EDWARD STONE it read in black paint on the mailbox, on Saturday morning, in a placid, mute snow that had only just begun to fall tentatively. And the old man trudged out toward me as I came up the dirt path to the cabin—moss-backed bleached siding, lattice-framed porch, drifts of gray chimney smoke furling over a high gable—a thick coil of manila rope slung over one shoulder and the ever-cold, ever-emberless pipe veering slantwise now, aiming west as he came north by northwest to front me at the corner of the covered garage.

Ed Stone's wasn't much of a spread. His farmhouse was gone, near-obliterated and fell-to-ruin—charred floor joists stubbornly parallel; a broken granite footing scattered now in among black riddled plumbing pipe warped and tempered in the sear of a firestorm; a haphazard square of dark rubble and cloven rock and scored chunks of beam heaped on the last vestiges of a hearth that had crumbled; and a tumbling half-wall of chimney stones. Two out-barns were stripped to the rafters, their siding strewn in among surrounding pines, the home pasture grown over with seedlings and wild stickerbrush and falling away to the south now in disarray, abandoned utterly to time and the seasons. As for the pineboard cabin—built on a regrade that sloped to a vale of ice and grim maple third-growth—it stood darkly back in shadows, tiny square windows opening out over lost pasture and the crossbuck door opening out onto stubble and ruin.

Dusting the snow from my shoulders I fell in and followed Ed Stone—*up this a way, Harper, now step along*—past his woodshed and barren chicken coop among pines until, twenty-five feet beyond the gable end of his home, he drew up and pointed ninety feet into the fragile, reaching branches of an American elm snapped like a pencil fifty feet up and slanting another forty into the forked branches of a slender tamarack: where it waited, wavering, half-toppled and leafless, for another storm wind to send it hurtling down like a battering ram launched by the gods to split asunder Ed Stone's dark cabin.

In the half-light of morning—outlined against the pines and the gray geometry of his ruins—the old man looked as twisted and tremulous and inexorably muted as the lost trodden silent figures I moved among for pay at the shadowed Burrillville Sanatorium. His spectacles were askew and the checked mackinaw buttoned unevenly so that one side of the collar rode higher than the other, absurdly prominent. Ed Stone stood half-bent-over backward, dark spittle frozen at the corner of his lips, the skin of his neck translucent, cold-blue, his hollowed face worked tight against the tiny stabbing needles of new snow, and peering, pipestem wavering, breath wheezing forth like dust from a clogged bellows, up through spotted glass at the broken shaft of the elm hung high above, one unlikely horizontal—a ford-bridge spanning far reaches of the trees—in a grove of true vertical pines.

"Trick is," he said, freeing his arm from the coil of manila rope, "to get that thing down 'thout caving the house in 'ta same time."

And with that he commenced to render his plan in the hard language of oratory—as though, instead of pulling back and toppling over a jammed windfall, we were preparing to cross the Delaware and meet the Hessians at Trenton on Christmas Day. When he ceased I dropped the coil of rope over my neck and climbed through the branches of a pitch pine per instruction, sculpted a weight-knot and flung it out over the bole of the elm in question, watched it un-ravel earthward—Ed Stone lashing a second coil to it fifty feet down—reeled both back in like well cable and ran the free end over the opposite side. The double rope hung now with both ends at ground level, draped over the shaft of the elm, and Ed Stone crafted some kind of hitch in it unsteadily while I wrestled my way out of the pitch pine and glanced out over the chaotic pasture and the trapezoidal jumble of bleak farmhouse ruins.

Snow, like a film of white dust, had begun to gather in arcs and depressions, wherever the canopy of branches over-head did not shield and sift, along the pathway that ran from the ruins to the crossbuck door and then to the covered garage, in chalklines over the spines of green exposed branches and on the steep-pitched roof and highest chim-ney stones of the dark cabin, and in a spangling bright coat over the surface of the ruins, the scattered, skewed footing and naked, dancing pipe, the coal-black, charred beams, the rails of joists, the remnant-rafters and chunk-wood clutter-ing the last of the cold stone hearth. The earliest, true, unfail-ing snow of winter had begun in earnest, picking up as the gray light it fell out of rolled along the backs of the clouds, slowly grew, and refracted back into the heavens again—a suggestion of earthly, naked and familiar light only beyond the crowns of Ed Stone's trees.

I didn't see it—though I have seen it in memory—when the old man took his tumble at the cornerstone of his im-placable ruins. I'd left him behind me in his grove of dark trees and gone down to bring his pickup around according to our prospectus for battle—left him paying out rope, back-ing up stiltingly between the pines with his head cocked toward the gray light, the rude hitch he'd built flowing up toward the bole of the elm, flowing at first and then floundering and wobbling at a shallower slant as he hobbled backward: finally, unwitnessed, the fall itself, a chance, solitary thing, and then—muffled and powerless—his cry in the snowfall.

I turned and wheeled up the path again, alone with a suddenness that made my breathing seem to echo inside my ears, and found Ed Stone pawing at the edge of his farmhouse ruins, a grimace of astonishment and rue and self-exacerbating vexation sculpted onto his drawn features, his steel-rims cockeyed, haywire, his familiar pipe—as much a part of him as his fingers and hands—nowhere to be found, and the manila rope, like a pendulum dying out, swinging at the merest arc ten feet in front of him through the snowfall. Grimly, obscenely determined, awkward and grotesque—like a plowhorse who has snapped a foreleg and, writhing, lathered, cannot accept or understand the meaning of proneness, of gravity and earth pounding him down—the old man waggled upward, clenching bits of jagged stone between his gloved fingers and rising, flopping, searching inwardly for a way to find a foothold and stand upright. A new look came over him, a seizure of pain engulfed him, lit his eyes and face—old fool that he was, he'd brought his weight down on the left fibula, the bone he'd cracked going over backward—and Ed Stone slipped down on his side, folded together like brittle paper, and clutched his broken leg tightly and cried without shame where he lay amid the old snowy ruins.

I lifted him gently—light as a newborn calf—and carried him, cradled him like a lamb, one arm across the backs of his knees and the other under his shoulder blades, careful of the leg turned unnaturally outward, up toward the warm heart of his cabin. Through the clean smell of snow his close, pungent smell came at me: the leaves of an old book, Mason jars in a cellar, dried mushrooms and toothpaste. The old man whimpered and wept tears that touched me with a perplexed guilt and shame, not two feet from my face as I held him in my arms, his eyes spinning wetly behind their thick lenses, weeping without courage of any kind which seemed then incomprehensible, impossible.

Inside the stove was nearly out, the cabin dark as a cave, bitter with the acrid smell of wood smoke. I let the old man slowly down on the sheets of his unmade bed in the corner alcove of the single room, where he fell limp, breathing roughly, and gazed up stiffly at the black soot that lay like paste over the ceiling beams. I rang up the doctor in Wilkes in a time when house calls were still possible, and yelled into the receiver—which crackled back at me—and then I hung up and waited without words for what had happened, listening to a clock somewhere that kept deafening time—*click-clack, click-clack*—and stoking the stove with sticks of maple.

"Do you want a blanket on?" I asked when the fire was drawing good.

"No. I don't need any blanket."

"You need anything?"

"Go on home, boy. Job's finished."

I sat down at his dining table.

"Doctor's coming," I said. "I'll wait 'til then."

The old man grunted and lapsed into silence in his corner.

Fifty minutes later Doc Schofield set the leg. Around noon Vic Crowell showed from up the Vaughan Road and pulled the snapped elm over with his snowplow. It hammered down into the ruins and I brought out the old man's chain-saw and bucked it up into lengths for the fire.

At two-thirty Ed Stone's son pulled in from West Putnam, Connecticut, where he was chief of the fire department. He asked me what happened. I told him everything. He gave me five dollars and I trudged home through the gray light of the woods.

~~~~~~~~~~~~~~~

Spring came, not dolorous and unassuming as it comes where I live now, but delirious and ravenous and unbridled, with blaring sunlight.

At the sanatorium the response to this change was min-ute, a meditation only on light and leaf buds and green thrusting grass, on wind as ally now and not enemy. All sense of the celebratory was muted by a felt continuity in all things, for life there was beyond the seasons, or so it appeared to me, wheeling my charges out to the shore of Harrow's Pond where the green bloom of marshweed and the sun on black water seemed to speak to me alone among the silent old ones. Leaves returned to the trees one day when no one watched, the earth softened, larks fluttered over the surface of the pond, but the marks of passing time there remained constant, fixed in perpetuity, ignorant of season and of the trajectory of sunlight. Someone died in bed, like Mrs. Curfall, who slept with her needleworked handbag at her side, curled beneath the sheets no larger than a ten-year-old child; or someone transferred quietly to a hospital in Boston, like Mr. Oslough, whose goiter stran-gled him with every utterance, maliciously; or someone else achieved a small victory like an arrangement of flowers or a painting of the pond or a group completed a long tournament of canasta and drank tea with mock-smiles on their faces; or, like Mrs. Tullis—who was taller than I in her eighties and nearly hairless, grave-faced and mute—someone died abruptly, pitched forward and did not rise again while the rest looked on without words for what they had seen. And thus time marked itself at the sanatorium, elegiacally.

It was a bright keen morning in late May when I saw Ed Stone again, five months after his sudden fall at the corner of the old ruins. I stood beside Mrs. Kennaugh at the shore of Harrow's Pond, where she slept profoundly in her wheelchair with her mouth dropped open —eyeballs leaping behind their pasty lids, her endless knitting, needles embedded eternally, dangling from her lap—and Ed Stone, Jr., fire chief from West Putnam, wheeled his old father down the path that wound through the pine grove and ended at pond's edge. He stopped, and drew the brake up, and stood behind him and beside me, arms snugly crossed, feet planted wide, while the old man, expressionless, with a face blank as slate, sat with his shoes askew on the footrest and looked out over the black water. "Storm coming," the son said—old himself from where I looked on, burly and kindfaced, with a belly like a cast-iron stove—and pointed—jammed—a finger into the west where thunderheads were piling up on the horizon. The light over the pond fell full and golden, a lucid, towering radiance as though bits of the sun itself were bursting out of the sky overhead, but in the west, far enough off so that it appeared to be something of a mirage, a grayness was gathering.

To me Ed Stone appeared smaller all over, his shirt front loose as a sack, his spectacles perched on his nose precariously, his ankles, sheathed in dark socks, as thin as stilts where they disappeared into his shoes. His features, in profile, seemed sallow and deflated as he stared down beneath the surface of the pond with his spotted hands trembling on his knees, chewing his gums laboriously. He had the seated posture of a man made delicately of powder, as though with the first good wind he would collapse into mist, like a puffball gone to seed, and float out over the pond in a cloud of dust, leaving his shirt and shoes and trousers heaped in the wheelchair. There was no pipe, and the teeth were missing, forgotten or useless; the entire lower portion of his face had caved in around the hole of his mouth. The veins in the temples looked flatter, darker, the face itself less stern and more preoccupied. He seemed accustomed to—though it was clear in the rigid line of his body not accepting of— moving through the world in a seated position, pushed from behind by a force that was not of his own making. Beneath the spectacles his eyes swam as nervously as minnows.

"We'll have to get your rod down, Dad," the son said heartily, locking his hand over the old man's shoulder. "Plenty of bass in this pond."

Mrs. Kennaugh stirred, wheezing, her breathing troubled briefly, and her head lolled down onto her left shoulder. An orderly from another unit passed wheeling a child, a girl of twelve or so who foamed at the mouth as she rolled down the path, gesticulating wildly and gibbering in some garbled, private language, cryptic and guttural, revolving her hands at the sun. They stopped twenty yards farther along the shoreline, and the orderly began to skip stones lightly over the surface of the pond. The girl, belted tightly, pale forearms beating furiously past her ears, cheered madly at each expert toss, driven by a secret beneficent rapture she alone could comprehend. Across the pond a canvasback skittered over the surface of the lily pads, and ducking beneath the skin of the water—sleek, soundlessly—disappeared into the blackness.

At noon I brought the old man dinner in the room he'd come to share with Mr. Lloyd, near the end of the third-floor corridor. He sat alone, turned toward the shadowed light of his cell's single window, as spare and plain and unmoving as the gray tubular bedsteads and the washstand and the squat bedside table where I saw now his pipe, his teeth at the bottom of a spotted waterglass, and a black case for his spectacles. Mr. Lloyd, poor eyes turned to the ceiling, lay in bed with the sheet pulled up to his chin, staring at nothing in particular and massaging the thick veins in his forehead with patient deliberation. Three or four flies hummed in a tight circle over him, but Mr. Lloyd seemed not to notice, and so even the flies became a part of the burden of stillness that had come to oppress their room.

"Is it breakfast?" Mr. Lloyd asked. "Too early for breakfast. Robert's coming, I think. We're going home."

I folded back his sheets, lifted the catheter tube, and removed the bedpan.

"I'm bringing the washbasin," I said. "Mr. Stone, do you need to use the lavatory before you eat?"

His head swiveled, quavering, and his eyes, red-rimmed in the gray light, flamed with sad recognition and with a pride distilled by my presence and by my question. His lips drew back toward a configuration of reproach—it was I who had trespassed last winter, after all—which was unattainable without teeth as a bulwark. Ed Stone pried his wheelchair around and faced me, then rolled over to the bedside table and locked his teeth in snugly, carefully. "Lavatory," he said, tugging on the front molars. "Lavatory? Is that what you're askin' about, boy?"

"Yes, sir," I said. "I'm going down there to empty this bedpan and you might as well come along if you need to."

Mr. Lloyd raised his head off the pillow and said, "Is that Robert coming? I hear good, you know. Do you see this? I can ring for the nurse with this gadget. She's a busy girl."

I raised his catheter tube again, pressed it into the cinch at the edge of a fresh bedpan, and turned the sheets down.

"Thank you, kindly," Mr. Lloyd said.

"You're welcome."

In the doorway I turned and looked over my shoulder. "Coming?" I asked.

Ed Stone sat clutching the armrests of his wheelchair, and then his fingers edged to the wheel rims and he revolved himself studiously toward me, head down. "No, I'm not coming," he answered from the foot of his bed, and wheeled to the single gray window again, where he halted, trembling, and stared out.

Mr. Lloyd let his head fall back and began to knead his blackened temples once more.

"Suit yourself, folks," he said to the ceiling, to the flies spinning over him, to nobody and nothing in particular. "Everybody—suit yourself. Go right ahead. Feel free."

Thunder bellowed in the distance—the west storm coming in from Connecticut. A robin lighted on the sill beyond the pane of glass. It shimmered, hopped twice, weightless and bobbing, head twitching fragilely not a foot from Ed Stone's eyes, and then floated out among the pines.

~~~~~~~~~~~~~~~

In the morning they found him face up beneath the surface of Harrow's Pond, bound in the marshweed, eyes wide and staring out into the sun and clouds. He'd left the wheelchair at the edge of the path, sometime in the night beneath stars that glistened after the storm had thundered by, and hobbled on crutches to the south shore, where he took his spectacles off and placed them under a sapling pine, folding them neatly on a bed of needles, and leaned his crutches up against the slender bole in the moonlight. Quietly he'd freed himself of his mackinaw, the one so identical to mine—I have it still, my son wears it fishing—and draped it over a low bough with his pipe and pouch in the breast pockets, and stood at the border of the grove with the pond before him, shivering because the night air closed him in. Barefoot—the black Hitchcocks, socks stuffed in their toes, left behind on the gravel—he'd crawled into the cold and swam with his bad leg dangling useless in the deeper water, pushing the surface back and making for the frigid heart of the pond. At last—and it was swift, and the old man felt breathless when it happened—he reached a place where there was no decision, the lights in the sky fell away and he was dropping effortless through a shroud, a womb, the surface receded before him impossibly, irrevocably, and yet it *receded,* it was as he had made it, it was farther away already while he noted it, and it was something like moving down a tunnel in a dream, with time, even, to note the sensation of thought without breath—the thought of no breath, how unacceptable and queer—and in a swirl that contained him bottomlessly he pondered what might be the right last thoughts to have and they were all of them, all of them, trivial, especially the pondering itself, and its triviality trivial even, and that was the last, from within his paralysis of body he no longer noted anything, only that there was no light to speak of, or that everything, somehow, was brilliantly lit, the light and the darkness one, united—and finally even that disappeared.

Arcturus

At the Last Stop Grocery Carl James pulled over. "Will you look there?" he said to his wife.

Four teenagers were drinking beer and squatting against the Last Stop's wall. They had a case of Hamm's in front of them and they were smoking cigarettes and looking at the highway.

I know the score with these here fellows, Carl said to himself.

"We need a couple things for tonight," he told his wife, getting out and peering through the windowframe of their camper, then rubbing the small of his back with his fingertips because the drive from town had been a long one. "Do you want maybe anything in here?"

Louise set her knitting in her lap and answered, "I guess I packed what we need already. But why don't you pick up some cookies, maybe? We can eat them tonight while we're playing cards."

A teenager with no shirt on, his chest muscles glowing, walked past them carrying a case of beer in his arms.

"Cookies," Carl said to his wife. "Any special kind?"

"Nope," Louise said.

"You sure?" Carl asked. "You don't want your coconut ones?"

"Nope," Louise insisted. "Surprise me this time."

Carl said, "Will do. Wait right here."

As he walked past the teenagers Carl heard himself say, "Don't drink 'em all in one snort now, fellas. You're liable to pass out doing that."

He regretted it immediately. It was just the kind of thing, he knew, that he should never say to any young people.

"For sure," one of the teenagers answered.

Carl walked around the Last Stop getting what he needed. By the time he made it to the rear of the store he had a large watermelon, a bag of Cheese Flips, a can of baked beans, and a half-case of beer in his cart. He planned to drink the beer along with a small flask of scotch he had hidden in his tackle box, to sit by himself on the bank of the Little Nelson River, listening to the water splash by and getting drunk one little piece at a time.

He went down the aisle toward the bakery goods, and that was when he saw Floyd Paxton—a red-faced fellow now, with a flowery Hawaiian shirt hanging over his belly like a curtain. *Floyd!* he almost said. But something stopped him. Floyd stood there panting a little and staring at the display of pies, cakes, tarts and doughnuts.

While Carl watched, Floyd scratched the red, bald crown of his head, cleared his throat in a thick rumble and picked out a boysenberry pie. He wore sandals and his toenails looked rotted. When he burped silently his lips curled back, and Carl saw that his teeth had rotted too. Everything about Floyd was old, loused up and rusty. Still, it was Floyd all right. Carl understood that perfectly. It was Floyd after many, many years, was all. It was Floyd, a fat old man.

Jesus, Carl said to himself. *I don't want to see this. Jesus Christ.*

Floyd stacked two pies on top of the boysenberry, then shuffled away toward the meat section of the Last Stop.

Jesus, Carl said silently again. *No.*

He paid for his things and went outside. It was a hot afternoon, a Friday in August; more teenagers had arrived. Two of them drank beer in the cab of a pickup, rock music spilling from the windowframes.

"What's up?" one of them said to him.

"Nothing much," Carl answered, his voice wavering.

He stowed the bag of groceries, his beer and the watermelon. "I forgot your cookies," Carl explained to Louise when he had their camper rolling again. "I'm sorry, but I just plain forgot is all."

Louise had her knitting going good now. The needles were flashing in the sunlight coming through the windshield.

She said, "It's all for the best. We didn't need them anyway."

"Not unless we want to become a couple of fat people," said Carl.

"Isn't it the truth?" Louise answered. "Except only we already *are* fat people. I am, leastwise, and you're getting there, Carl."

She poked a forefinger into the side of Carl's gut. Carl slapped it away, laughing.

"Hey," he said. "You're not fat. You look fine, Louise."

"Eat right, get plenty of exercise, and take Geritol," Louise said seriously.

They both laughed then. They were entering the woods along the river. Carl saw the sign that said NORTH FORK CAMPGROUND 14 MILES.

Carl had helped build the forms one summer for the fire-pits at the North Fork Campground. He'd poured the concrete. He'd cleared the campsites. He'd helped dig the holes for the outhouses. Floyd, too.

They were only teenagers then, Floyd and himself, but they were working already, working in the woods, doing what they could to get along.

That summer they'd gotten on with a government work crew. They worked on Forest Service land—building stick piles and burning them, or digging fire line and laying hose on it—whatever the crew boss said, they did.

They'd worked along the banks of the Little Nelson sometimes.

After work they'd generally pulled over at the Last Stop for a few bottles of Blue Ribbon. They had a house, Floyd and Carl, at the edge of an old apple orchard at the foot of the mountains, and they would go there and eat bologna sandwiches for dinner. Sometimes they would swim in the Deer Pool on the Little Nelson, or they would sit in front of the Last Stop together, drinking beer in the sun, bothering the same girls they'd bothered at the high school, smoking cigarettes and watching the cars and logging trucks go past.

But this was all years ago, long before Carl moved away to Seattle and went to work at the Boeing Company. He'd done everything there. He'd been through a lot since then. He'd fought in two wars, for example. His daughters were grown up, married, and had children. His first wife had died of cancer in her lymph nodes, and Carl had married Louise. He'd met her at the Food Circus—they ate tacos, then danced the polka. Her husband had died from a stroke, she told him. When they were engaged he sent Floyd Paxton an invitation, but Floyd had never written back or responded. Perhaps he was dead, Carl'd said to himself. So he forgot about Floyd Paxton. It had been a long, long time ago, really, and there was no point in always looking backward.

But now he remembered almost despite himself. On a Saturday back then they'd taken their inner tubes up and put them in the Little Nelson River. Carl drank his fifth beer of the day in water up to his thighs. Floyd was on his fifth beer, too. They stood there holding their tubes against the current, naked, with flat stomachs, drinking beer beneath a fragile blue sky.

"Here we come, river!" Floyd had yelled, lofting his beer bottle into the forest.

He took the remaining beers and laid them inside a burlap sack. He lashed the sack to his inner tube with a section of manila rope. It was a day of no wind, bright and hot, in high country, virgin forest, and the river ran along through there steep and recklessly.

"Five beers makes you immune to pain," Floyd explained. "If you smash your head on a rock downriver you aren't even going to notice it."

"Good," said Carl. "Then we're okay."

"We're okay," Floyd agreed. "Still, we got these extra beers here just in case. And an opener. For emergency situations."

He pulled the dripping burlap sack out of the water, grinning.

"Sort of like a first-aid kit," Carl said.

"Sort of," Floyd said. "You might say that. You might say that was the case."

They shoved out. The river took them, gently at first, but unstoppable, Carl realized. The straight trunks of strong pine trees rose around them; sun glinted off snow in the high far mountains; the inner tubes carried them over the surface of the Little Nelson and the sun kept their bellies warm. When they came to places where boulders had fallen out of sheer hillsides they beat their hands against the current until the inner tubes began to revolve. That way, anything they hit they'd bounce off of.

They rode along. Their tubes caromed off of one another. Floyd's nose had gotten sunburned already, but he didn't seem to notice at all. They rolled over the water effortlessly, as in a dream, flowing around obstacles, ignorant not so much of imminent danger as of the weakness and smallness of human beings. The current kept them together in this: a pair of spilling, rushing teenagers.

They went through their first set of real rapids. Floyd yelled his way through the white water. Carl felt himself lifted from his inner tube. Under the water it was unsettlingly quiet, impossible to tell which way was up.

Jesus Christ, Carl'd said to himself.

It was beautiful and terrible all at once. His thigh smashed against a rock. His back smashed against something, too. He was moving too fast now. Tiny bubbles were everywhere. The silence was complete, he was rolling along underneath the river now, or inside of it rather, and here was a true view of how things went, he told himself, here was what the river was in its secret truth. He had no control anymore.

When he came up at last—out of nowhere, as if by

magic—his tube was a little bit ahead of him. He caught up with it, levered himself on, and rode downriver again in the white-yellow sunlight.

"Hey, Floyd!" he screamed out happily, ecstatically, over the screaming, tumbling white water.

Carl drove into second-growth forest. The pavement ended and the gravel began, popping underneath the tires. They curled around a wide bend now, and through the trees Carl saw the Little Nelson sparkling.

"There she blows," he said. "Look through the trees there, Louise."

Louise peered up from her knitting. She had a sweater three-quarters finished in her lap, something for the grand-daughter of some friends they played bridge with. The sweater had pine trees and reindeer knitted into it—exactly the right thing for a girl's Christmas gift. But the girl, Carl knew, wouldn't appreciate it. She was away at college, some-where in the East, where it was impossible for her to know about a thing like that.

"I don't see any river," Louise said, peering through the passenger-side window, needles fixed in midair.

At the North Fork Campground Louise undid her seat belt, then stood where Carl could see her in the side mirror—blinking behind her glasses at him, no doubt. He backed the camper neatly into its spot, Louise directing him with the utmost seriousness between the thick trunks of Douglas fir trees. With her hands waving the way he'd taught her she looked like one of those fellows on the deck of an aircraft carrier, and in the small disc of his one hundred and eighty degree mirror she appeared as some kind of hallucinated monster gesticulating to a sunset that couldn't care less. But that was all right. His first wife had never gone camping at all. In the old days he'd hiked into the back country, a fisherman. His first wife had often been moody about that, but when he came home she'd been happy to see him. The cancer in her lymph nodes had killed her slowly. Three years, all told, it took for her to die. He had seen men die in the snows of the Hunsrück, seen boys blown apart in Korea, then come home to watch his wife die.

He had married Louise to have some company—he knew that, so did she. It was true that she was overweight, she was nothing to look at, but what difference could that make to anyone? He had come, quickly, to be fond of her, inexplicably, and he knew she wouldn't betray him in any way, or demand things, or impinge. She had her own simple pleasures. Knitting, for example.

"I'm going down along the riverbank," Carl told her when the camper was leveled and blocked up on two-by-fours, the gas line hooked up, the water tank filled. "I'll be back in two shakes of a leg."

Louise said, "Well, be back in a jiffy then. I'm going to get busy here and put supper on."

She smiled at her husband. She squeezed Carl's forearm. "Anything wrong?" she asked.

"Not really," Carl answered.

"Well, don't jump in down there."

"I won't," Carl said. "I'm too old to jump."

They both laughed at that. Carl put the flask of scotch in his pocket and wandered out into the fir trees.

They'd gone over two little waterfalls. The descent from the high country was too fast, too sudden: impossible to make sense of, slipping past, slipping behind. Carl fell from his inner tube twice more, Floyd twice altogether. Past the canyon below Pinto Rock they'd pulled up on a sandbank and stretched out in the heat of the sun. Carl thought hard about things. He was drunk and the river was dangerous. Three of the beer bottles had been smashed in the rapids, but that left nine between the two of them.

They got up and floated on together. There was nothing quite like it, Carl decided, utterly happy with himself. There were stretches where they laid back with their hands behind their heads and stared up into the mountaintops circling the valley. In the bends the tubes seemed to seek out deep water—wherever the current went, they went. It was magical, the water deeply cold and swarming with light, the air unruffled and warm. The sun, though, had moved noticeably lower toward the mountains in the western sky.

Until now they'd seen no one, not even fishermen.

They bobbed down into the slower water beyond the North Fork, past the place where the North Fork and Middle Fork meet. They opened two beers and floated along with bottles in hand, watching the bank at the campground.

"Look at that," Floyd said.

Families were camped there. People suddenly. Kids ran among the trees. There were picnic tables covered with checkered picnic cloths. There were cars and women holding babies. A boy, fourteen or so, watched them longingly from the end of a spruce log that had fallen into the current. People sat in the sun above the cutbank, eating hot dogs and looking at the watercourse.

"Jesus," Carl said, feeling his nakedness all of a sudden. "We're down at the campground already."

"How can it be?" Floyd answered.

They floated on, right past the campground, past the sorry people huddled there, down where the river was broad and quiet.

"So long, suckers!" Floyd had yelled.

"Christ Jesus," Carl whispered.

He was too drunk now. His thigh felt numb and unserviceable where he had smashed it. Everything was changing. Everything was different. The water was a green color now full of mud and gick and slime—deep and sullen water, ugly water. There were bugs suddenly. The tubes moved very slowly. On either side of them stood silent willow trees.

"Hey," Carl said. "Let's get out of here. Let's go back." But then it occurred to him that to travel upstream was not likely or hardly even possible.

"Let's finish the beers first," Floyd insisted.

He hauled the burlap sack up between his legs and settled it onto his belly, dripping.

"Five left," he said. "Three for you and three for me."

They drank, dutifully. It was intensely quiet in the low country, quiet and hot, quiet, slow and lanquid, too still. Carl felt the tight pain of the sunburn in his shoulders. The only sound was the buzzing of the deer flies.

"Give me another," Carl said after a while. But he was only drinking now because he had to.

He opened his bottle—and then, because they had worked together all summer in the forest, and because their journey downriver was nearly over, because they had gone fishing together and lived in the same house at the edge of the mountains, because of a lot of things, not the least of which was the fact that Carl was as drunk as he had ever been, he told Floyd now that he would die for him.

"Did you know that, Floyd?" he said—overprecise about it, too drunk. "I'd die for you. If I ever had to. I mean in the war or something. I'd *die* for you. Just so's you know."

"Same here," Floyd insisted from his tube. "Me too, Carl. The same goes for me, just for the record, buddy."

They made a blood pact in the shallows. They cut their palms open with a broken bottle and shook hands like soldiers, swearing. "I'd die for you. I swear it. God damn it," Carl said. "Hell yes," Floyd had answered.

They were too drunk to feel embarrassed just then. And they didn't know any better anyway. They would only feel embarrassed sometime long afterwards—Carl for a long time, long after he'd gone to Seattle, long after everything else in his life had changed.

The river kept getting wider and slower—as if the flatland accepted it only grudgingly. Carl saw backwaters, eddies, marshes and pools—all the complications of a great river. The sun fell lower, the air turned oppressive. There were no trees now. There was marsh and marshweed at first, and then blackberry bush, and finally they came out into cultivated wheat fields, where farmers rode in rows on combines taking in the summer wheat.

At last the river turned into a lake—an enormous void of still water. And then they were *in* the lake, a dam at its end, in plain sight not far off.

~~~~~~~~~~~~~~~

After supper, after the dishes were cleared away, Carl went once again to the riverbank. He settled down with his back against a log and looked at the water aimlessly. What was there to see? He drank his scotch in sudden draughts, like medicine, bravely. He drank most of it. He had a beer in his jacket pocket, so he drank that, too.

He got up and found a boulder above the cutbank. He sat there, looking out at the places where he and Floyd had floated past with their drunken curses, down toward where they'd made their drunken vows, up into the bend where the two forks meet, toward the high roaring stretch of river where they'd begun their journey together. It had been a sweet journey, he thought now. He didn't want to forget about it ever. Even the ridiculous promises had been sweet. He *would* have died for Floyd back then. He'd been dumb enough and young enough for ridiculous things.

But now it was night, years later. The sun had set already, the stars were out—pinpricks in the overwhelming darkness of the skies. On the opposite bank a grove of birches had been cut down by spring runoff. Now the whole grove lay half in the river, a jumble of sticks rotting slowly and only barely reflecting the wild watercourse.

Straight above him Carl recognized Arcturus, the star in the middle of the heavens.

Nothing is going to change here, Carl thought—even though most things had changed already. And he wished he had never seen Floyd in the pie section. He wished it had never happened. Nobody needed that kind of reminder. Nobody deserved a jolt like that.

He went in. He and Louise sat at the table playing rummy and eating Cheese Flips. They played eight games before Louise took up her knitting again. Carl drank two cans of beer, slowly. They spoke of his daughters for a while—one was separated from her husband. Her husband was filing for divorce for some reason. Carl had not understood it. His daughter had called from somewhere in Wisconsin. A small town where a friend of hers lived.

He checked the gas before he got into bed. It was a Saturday night, ten o'clock, in August. The campground was chock-full: music and voices, cars rumbling by, people laughing as they moved toward the toilets behind their flashlight beams. Carl listened hard for the sound of the river, but the river was too far from there—one hundred yards, at least, through the fir trees.

They'd arrived late and taken one of the poorer campsites, far from the music of the Little Nelson. Carl regretted that now.

In bed Louise kissed him on the jaw, twice. "Cheer up," she said. "You'll go fishing tomorrow, Carl. Cheer up now, all right?"

He told her that he loved her. "I'd be lonely as hell without you," he said. He kissed her ear, her nose.

"You've been drinking whiskey," Louise answered. "You've been drinking and now you're full of bologna, Carl."

Carl was a light sleeper. It was his habit to stay up and worry nights. In fact, it seemed to him he hardly slept anymore; he couldn't seem to get the hang of it. And there was that picture in his head of Floyd at the Last Stop. Maybe he should have said something after all. Maybe Floyd would have known how to explain things.

He sat up, grunting, and pulled his pants on. He was still drunk, too drunk to lay in one place at least. He tied his shoes in the dark. He pulled his jacket on and went out with the flashlight. He made his way between the fir trees, stumbling once on a dead branch, fumbling a little in the clammy darkness, until he'd made his way down to the edge of the

Little Nelson River, where he stood listening to the endlessness of it.

Floyd! he said to himself. *Floyd! Jesus Christ!* But then he looked above him and there was Arcturus, Arcturus and about a million other stars, all shining in their mysterious way.

It made him feel better, seeing that. *Let the river rush and pour,* he thought; a river is a very small thing beside a star, after all. There were no words for it he could utter to himself, except that a star seemed the right sort of solace for a man going on seventy.

The Flower Garden

When I was young—seventeen—I had a paper route which I remember as a meandering through early summer, a ritual pilgrimage along old broad streets beneath maples just shooting out a soft haze of fresh buds. With my papers in their drapesack striking off my back and belly, and with a thick load of rubber bands coiled over my knuckles, I'd hike alone across the east side of town, rolling my papers tightly in thirds as I went and tossing them high in delicate arcs to land lightly in doorways and on porch steps. My route took me where the homes were large and venerable and still, where the lawns were broad and insistently mani-cured beneath the new-budding maples. Wherever I went, timeworn and meditative old men stood by and watched me behind the glitter of sprinklers, or pulled weeds mutely with a bland concentration, and plump-armed women in cotton dresses and tough black shoes hovered busily under clotheslines, dropping white sheets into deep wicker baskets. From eyes made large and watery by spectacles they watched me half-amused, half-sad and sentimentally, the women with wooden clothespins in their mouths, the men clutching garden spades and weeding forks or lawn rakes. As I walked I would catch the hot fruit sugar fragrance of the pies that baked in their kitchens, or the powdered soap smell of the drying sheets, or the mint-and-tinder scent of lawns mowed too often, and I would hear the lazy clinking of occasional wind chimes. Hummingbirds and blue jays gathered at feeders and a gold light fell out of a blue sky, intensifying, somehow, the stillness in everything.

When the drapesack was empty I flew home, knocked the dust from my cleats, rubbed neat's-foot oil into the soft heart of my glove—checking to see that its webbing was cinched tightly—and then I pulled my cap down low and ran up to Adams Field, where the Cardinals worked out through the late afternoon, where I stretched and warmed up and threw batting practice while the infield dust drifted low across the bleachers and the clean white chalklines were erased by the base runners. The catcher in his shinguards and facemask and chestpad sent me signals from under his well-worn glove. I learned to throw a breaking ball hard that summer; I got my slider down, privately dreaming of a shot at the majors, and followed Whitey Ford, Warren Spahn and Don Drysdale in the boxes. The sun flooded richly over the backstop and diamond, and when I turned to watch the high flies crest in the outfield a halo of pink light engulfed the spinning ball. I saw little else but what could be seen from the pitcher's mound at Adams Field. The view from there was of the game whirling magically around me, holding me delicately in its order and process and symmetry and motion, a fragile web of rule and action—myself at its center—that fended the world off perfectly, thwarted it completely, muted its terror with something as simple as a drag bunt laid neatly out across the infield.

In July new houses were added to my route, and Anna Lewis—who had black ringlets of hair at the nape of her neck, and a pair of dark moles at the base of one cheek, and blue eyes that could not be disturbed by commotion—lived in one of them: a three-story white clapboard colonial near one end of Tullis Street, a tall shuttered house set back behind hedges. Sitting cross-legged on a bench made of cool gray stone beside a sundial on a tapering pedestal, she read *War and Peace* and *Persuasion* and *Dead Souls* in its flower garden, which bloomed from May until the end of September with at least sixty species of perennials.

That first day on Tullis Street I trudged up the flagstones beyond the clasped gate in the perfect hedge, wedging a paper together as I went and smelling the honeysuckle, and then in a bend in the garden path I came on Anna, who frowned gravely up at me from out of the pages of the book she cradled in both palms, thumbs weighing the pages down, blue eyes casting me in the mold of intruder, her face tanned a clear sharp brown and the black tangled gloss of her hair framed in yellow sunlight. All around her, in a half-moon surrounding the stone bench and sundial, were flowers in sloped beds that rose to a high picket fence; beach stones lined the garden paths, and shade trees grew where the paths converged, in the midst of the garden at a raised gazebo beside a miniature fountain. With Anna behind me I tossed my paper, lofted it onto the high, broad porch, then turned again and passed her on the flagstones. As I did she glanced up at me, and a smile of amusement formed beneath the frown; her face seemed strong and brown, broad from ear to ear and gleaming as she held her book shut, marking her place with a forefinger. While I watched her black hair seemed to ripple in the sunlight and her wary eyes moved to the book once more. She shook her head once, briskly, not lifting her eyes, and the mane of her hair spilled over her forehead like a woven shield, iridescent and beautiful.

I was struck there and then I know now—the point of something sharp seemed lodged against my breastbone—not so much by beauty or romance but by my need and a nudging dread of it: dread of everything I would have to say and do against my will and yet precisely as my will wished. I knew about war from the baseball diamond—the private, intimate war of pitcher and batter in which subtleties of action are either gratifying or horrible—but not of the inner battle in which, even at seventeen, we recognize within desire the necessity of suffering. That comprehension of possible loss—of compromise, perhaps—and Anna's beauty filled me as I stood there, though Anna was not exactly beautiful—the bones in her face were too large somehow, and the chin a bit too narrow—her beauty had no being unless you were me and the time twenty-one years ago.

"Looks like a nice spot to read," I pointed out, mostly because I was no master of words and yet words seemed necessary.

"It is nice," she said. "It's very nice."

There was that odd frown again, that sobriety and calm. I fell charmed by two traits: good posture and courteousness. They did me in as they had done in boys before me who in time had become husbands.

"What are you looking at?"

"This? *Madame Bovary.*"

She'd said it this way: *Ma-dahm Boo-vah-ree.* I only nodded, though. "I haven't read it," I admitted.

"It's worth reading," said Anna. "I love it."

"That's good," I answered and, because I'd lost the vaguest connection to my natural brand of thought, because my disorientation in her presence felt so horribly complete, I changed the subject instantly. "These flowers are something. They're everywhere."

She looked at me with an astonishment so subtle I noted it only as a refraction of light in her eyes, a drawing inward of the corners of her lips. She looked at me and let her forefinger slide from where all along it had been marking her place in *Madame Bovary.* Anna rose and loosed upon me a grace such as I had never witnessed, becoming as she emerged from her seated posture an extension of my pathetic and absurd delusions. All of that hair. The exactitude, the coolness of her back's repose. I noticed, too, the length of her fingers. She was a girl composed of striking odd details. Take them as a whole and nothing matched precisely.

"You like them?" she said.

"Sure. How can I help myself?"

"You do?"

"Of course." But I didn't, not especially. I was lost in a conversation that impelled itself beyond the boundaries of my true thoughts. I was merely talking, saying things that did not necessarily reflect what was in my heart, because I wanted to be speaking with her; I knew that much.

"They've been a job," said Anna. "Constant work. But if everyone helps, and you do a bit each day, and don't get behind or let them get ahead of you, you don't notice it. Let things go and it becomes a miserable chore."

"Like a lot of things," I said.

"Everything," Anna insisted. "So many things are like that." She smiled, somewhat sage, and then both of us lowered our eyes.

I can tell you how I left there: light-footed and ecstatic and sick to my stomach all at once, rolling my papers too tightly and conjuring up futures in which Anna and flowers figured prominently. Within that madness I began to run, leaping up stairways and crashing over lawns, flipping my papers at porches breathlessly while the old stony men in their yards looked on in silence, mystified, betrayed by memories that no longer reached back into boyhood.

This is how it went: I would find Anna in the garden almost daily, reading or culling bouquets or pinching the tops of the annuals off between her fingers, and on the days she was not there I felt strongly the weight of time, which seemed to languish between our encounters, and eventually she taught me the names of all the flowers and how to identify them in bloom—gaillardia, sedum, loosestrife, feverfew: one by one I came to know them separately, according to the shapes and colors of their petals, leaves and stems. It was the sort of esoterica I had never had an interest in but which now composed a whole world. We would linger at the stone bench, I would pull my drapesack of papers off, and Anna would put her book down and quiz me on the flowers I had memorized. We worked our way around the paths, kneeling at the beds beside the blooms, and there was something perfect and athletic, rolling, natural, in the way Anna's arms and hands moved through the plants and bushes, pushing stems back or cupping petals while the bees flew in and out among the stalks and leaves. The more carefully I noted her gentleness and the ease of her knowledge the more agitated I became, and I would eye her as I eyed the flowers, secretly. When I found her pulling weeds—balanced on the balls of her feet, crouching and leaning into the flower beds—she looked up at me with pinpricks of sweat along her hairline, where the skin was whiter, and the black tendrils at the base of her neck seemed slick and oily. She rose smoothly and brushed the dirt out of her summer dress—she wore one every day, and they were all many sizes too large—and then she clapped the dust from her hands and stood with her fingertips poised against her hips, looking out over the flower garden. She wore sandals bound behind the ankle and over the flank of the foot with flimsy straps, and her calves shone in the sun and her brown shoulders and neck shone, and she might scratch her throat or cheek thoughtfully, leaving a smudge of dirt behind, and then she moved down the path in that fluid yet controlled way of hers, smooth and long-boned and utterly at home among the flowers. And all of that made me sentimental, which I knew was a weakness but couldn't help.

Occasionally I saw Anna's mother—who was thin and narrow in the face, wore a gardening apron everywhere and parted her hair severely down the middle—moving along the flagstone paths and dragging a hose behind her, or darting about with a can full of fish fertilizer, and whenever our eyes met she smiled faintly and cryptically, but hardly ever said a word to me directly. Anna's father, Doctor Herbert Franklin Lewis, was thick and ruddy and wore coarse suits. On Saturday afternoons he worked in his garden, or sat in the gazebo with his heavy legs crossed and smoked a cigar meditatively, clutching a glass of iced tea between his hairy fingers and whistling unrecognizable tunes. He paid his bill for the newspaper promptly and tipped me twenty-five cents magnanimously, flicking his bow tie and caressing the great red wattles of skin that fell over his throat in separate flaps. He was a large, difficult and serious man who spoke to me often of the vagaries of baseball, wiping his face all around with a handkerchief and exuding a domestic, comfortable confidence. I often think of him now as one of a dying breed of men, who want, really, nothing for themselves, who have effaced their innermost desires without self-flagellation, and—in order to avoid the desperations of solitude—have given themselves over completely to their wives and to their children, and ultimately to their children's children, and done it with a magnificent serenity.

Mostly, though, Anna and I were alone in the garden, and I began to linger there, late for practice. Eventually we lay in the grass that fronted the gazebo, where one day I pressed myself over her at last, locked my forearms against her cheeks and curled my hands through her hair. She was pensive, uncertain, her face paled slightly and silence overtook her; she seemed to be studying my face, searching its features for a truth that stubbornly remained hidden, and her hands only rested below my shoulder blades, waiting and plaintive and still. In time, though, I saw that her eyes were no longer wary, and when I pressed myself over her I felt her back arch and her hips swell to meet mine. It was a form of paradise and I knew it even then: the depth of the sunlight as it glowed through the garden, the bitter, private, fleshy taste of Anna's lips and mouth, the warm abrasiveness of grass against my arms and legs, and the choking scent of flowers everywhere, all around us, shutting the world out forever.

Yet at times, at the core of bliss, I would feel a dread I'd never felt before; I would dream through my ears the clack of a bat, resonant and crystalline, but when I lifted my head up to listen for it, it ceased to exist altogether. My chest tightened, seized up in knots, and Anna peered into my eyes suspiciously: I got up suddenly and hurried away from there with my eyebrows knit and my jaw jutting, saying I was late for baseball practice. And, in hurrying away, alone and loping along the streets effortlessly, I felt a transformation taking place; the further I got from the flower garden and the closer to Adams Field, the more ecstatic I became, until before long Anna seemed like a dream, beautiful and tranquil and surrounded by flowers, but far from the stuff of which my real life was made. By the time I reached the pitcher's mound I felt no dread anymore, could not remember dread at all, and I would throw batting practice with a soaring heart, at the hub of the wheel of the baseball field.

That summer season came and went, the Pittsburgh Pirates won the World Series, the flowers knit themselves up against winter, and everywhere I took my papers that fall maple leaves rattled drily in the windy streets, curled like fists and skating in hordes along the asphalt. With school again—my last year of it—I brought the papers around at three; Anna was no longer in the garden (the air had turned too sharp and cold) but in the evenings I walked up and we sat by the fire with the television on softly and our schoolbooks open. Doctor Lewis hunkered down beside us in his thick padded armchair and eventually slept peacefully with a cold cigar between his fingers, and Mrs. Lewis seemed always to be

padding back and forth stealthily behind us in her slippers
and awkward chenille bathrobe. The wall clock ticked like
thunder and the fire popped and fizzled and Doctor Lewis
wheezed through one nostril and exhaled his breath like a
clogged bellows, and Anna and I leaned together in the calm
purple wash of the television's light, not asleep and not
awake, in a trance of sorts until the clock belled eleven and
the late-night news came on. With the news Doctor Lewis
stirred and perked up, lit his cigar again and watched in a
daze with his arms folded across his belly. "Sports report,"
he said to me. "Let's all be quiet now."

Irrelevant football scores perhaps, or meaningless trades
in distant cities, or the retirement of a gladiator no longer
filled with the requisite bravado, the requisite innocence
and awe. "He was a superb ath-alete," Doctor Lewis com-
mented on the occasion of some obscure player's slide from
the fields of glory. "Absolutely superb. A whiz."

On another occasion, as we sat through a round of advertisements, he waxed candidly prophetic. "Don't be frightened by failure, son," he warned me out of nowhere, from
no source—just sudden words spoken boldly. "The world is
filled with men who dream of their own importance. No,
don't be fooled by the prospect of failure. You've a fine, fine
arm. A fine arm. Who knows? The true loss would be in not
trying a 'tall, with one so young as you are. . . ." But I don't
think he knew how to finish, or even quite what he meant
to say. Doctor Lewis was a lost and sentimental man; he
went off to bed when the news was done without any further
advice. I had the sense that the confusion and mystery he'd
left me with were purposeful.

"What was he talking about?" I asked his too-lovely and
too-quiet daughter.

"Baseball." Just one word. Then: "You."

We talked for some time, with great seriousness, and about matters better left untouched by children. At last, because she'd implied for so long that the words were really necessary, I told Anna that I loved her. I said it with my head hung and my eyes averted. I remember there were icicles hanging from the eaves; it was just before Thanksgiving and the killing-frost had come and gone—she cupped my face in her hands as we sat side by side on her mother's sofa and—with eyes that were stern, wet and scared, eyes that were serious even about themselves—Anna said she loved me too, plainly and boldly and with too much painstakingly concocted drama for me not to feel ill about everything. She waited for me to fill the empty space that followed, to ladle emotion into it—staring at me, and me sick about it, sweating. I felt her breath on my face and smelled her clean flesh and just-washed hair—something like a tremor went through me which I suppressed and concealed while I made a comic face, a parody of lovesickness, a mask as reply, an image of what I kept myself from being or becoming—she didn't laugh and I flicked out the light behind us and kissed her with a force that I wished could obliterate the need for words but which failed to do so; I didn't know what I felt, not really, not well enough to articulate it anyway, and within my excesses of ecstasy and dread there was only turmoil and uncertainty about Anna. I knew that, suddenly, too well.

Later, walking home in the cold through streets that were dark but for the blurred glow of streetlamps, I felt relief at having a bed of my own to return to. At home I stared hard at the ceiling of my room, knowing what I felt and knowing it was a betrayal of feelings I had felt to be true until then: I squeezed my eyes shut until a thousand helixes of light shot forth inside them, and told myself I loved Anna a hundred times until somehow, in the silent utterance, it seemed to have become true and I could finally sleep.

A wave, though, had been set in motion. That winter I waited, mostly, for baseball season; I threw some, indoors, and I gave up my paper route to concentrate on pitching. When spring came my arm was already strong, and I had added a sweeping knuckleball to my repertoire. The ground thawed in a sudden rush of heat, the grass turned green in the field again and the team turned out in the afternoon beneath skies that were turquoise and empty of clouds. In the evenings I often showed up at the Lewises' and met Anna in the garden—reading, as always, at the stone bench—and it was then, in April, that we began to plant a slope of the yard with a few perennial flowers of our own.

I don't remember where the idea came from anymore, but no doubt it was Anna's: she was obsessed with gardening, with gardens and books about people who never lived by people who were no longer living. One evening, simply, I found myself busy with a hoe and rake, rooting up strips of lawn behind the gazebo. We plowed a long crescent of soil to a depth of twelve inches, and shoveled the earth through an angled rock screen, and then we tilled in four twenty-pound bags of steer manure and raked a clean contour into the bed. I spread a thin layer of vermiculite one Saturday and we sat down at the stone bench and made out our garden plan meticulously. We sketched in, along the edge of the lawn, Jacob's-coat, heliotrope, zinnias, astilbe, bearded iris, alyssum, baptisia, forget-me-nots and evening primroses. Behind these we added white regal lilies and pink phlox—late summer flowers—backed by a line of delicate snakeroot. Lastly, we filled in with gas plant and butterfly weed and a few day lilies—long-suffering flowers that will bloom even where there is no nurturing and little sustenance.

The sun fell behind the house while we planned and measured, and it became too dark to see our sketch easily. I went home, but all the next week, evenings, we planted with nursery sets and fragile garden cuttings, and raked over a layer of leaf mulch, shredded, in order to keep the weeds from taking root in the dark loose soil. By the middle of April—baseball season—Anna and I had a flower garden of our own to care for, and sometimes, as I waited to throw from the home dugout at Adams Field, I would wonder suddenly when the first blooms would begin to appear, and I wanted to be there when the buds began to open in the sun below the white gazebo.

That was a surprising, golden season—my last good season, really, in baseball (there is something, though, to be said to the good for my seasons as a spectator since then, too). My arm had hardened over the winter and I'd found my throwing strength at last; I learned to concentrate on the mound, to expurgate the unnecessary clutter of the world at game time, and when I got behind on a batter or had men on base I still kept my focus on the strike zone. I'd come to insist that the enclosed world of baseball protect me altogether finally, and as love became more difficult I probed the intricacies of pitching more deeply and perhaps more desperately, too. As long as the game lasted I was safe, hidden, but when it ended—when the season ended, I feared—I would come to myself in a shudder of self-knowledge and absorb the turmoil of love once more. It was a strategy of disciplined withdrawal, yes—how many athletes are driven by the confusions of their lives to do well at games?—but within it my numbers led the High School League: nine and one, sixty-five strikeouts, a two-point-three-one e.r.a. I pitched eight complete games—two of them three-hitters, three of them shutouts—and *The Clarion*—the newspaper I'd delivered on the east side once—wrote me up in June as a bona fide major league prospect.

Two days after graduation the Kansas City Athletics called. They wanted me in their farm system, at Chambers, upstate, for two-seventy-five a month plus per diem and bus fare and a chance to step right into the rotation or, if that didn't work out, a guaranteed spot in the bullpen. I told them yes immediately, that I would report in three days, and then I went over to see Anna Lewis, figuring in my head as I walked the time it would take before I was pitching in the big leagues.

It was a drowsy hot June afternoon, moist and sweltering and windless. At the stone bench in the flower garden you could smell the thick spice of clove pinks; behind the sundial you could see the red heads of bee balm thrusting up toward the heat of the sun. Anna's book—*Mansfield Park* this time—lay on its spine with the pages open; it seemed absurd and tiresome and petty in light of the Kansas City Athletics. I wound along the flagstones to the gazebo. From there I could see Anna kneeling at the border of our garden, dressed in her mother's dirt-stained gardening apron and with her hair crimped into a loose bun full of black tendrils. Black sprigs of hair fell away from her ears and her neck as she worked with a weeding spade along the sliver of astilbe we had planted, tossing the uprooted weeds behind her with a minute turn of the wrist. They lay limply behind her in a long broken row at the edge of the lawn slope, each with its own root-crust of earth crumbling into the green grass and drying to a listless gray hue in the heavy swelter.

Perennials—even nursery starts—come into their own only gradually, and seldom make much of a show before their second season. Our garden was too new and tender and therefore scarcely in flower; the best we could hope for was a few forget-me-nots and, perhaps late in summer, some pink phlox and a smatter of snakeroot. The astilbe, though, had miraculously bloomed—it was the middle of June already and nearing the solstice; the days had been long and hot and at dawn all month the sudden rains had come—and now they showed their feathery spires in a halo around Anna. I went down the lawn slope and began to gather up the pulled weeds. Sliding along with one knee in the grass and a clutter of weeds dangling from one fist I told Anna about Kansas City and Chambers and the two-seventy-five a month the Athletics would pay me to play baseball. My memory of this moment is clear—my life, in retrospect, seems to have turned on it—Anna rose and dusted off her apron, smacked the dirt from her hands and reached into the pocket of her summer dress. She held the envelope out to me; I let fall the tangle of weeds in my hand and sat back on the lawn to read what it contained.

A school in Pennsylvania—Saint Alphonse College—had offered Anna a full scholarship to study literature: now I knew what all her books fed into. I read the letter twice; halfway through the third reading I knew that she would go, that when the season ended in Chambers and I came home she would be gone, that when she returned the next summer I would be pitching somewhere else again and wanted to, and that this would go on endlessly and we would see

each other almost never, until at last we were entirely
strangers. I didn't know whether or not this was what I
wanted, whether dread or ecstasy ought finally to be the
state of things; I loved her as long as it was simple—as it was
in the flower garden—but now the sticky web of the larger
world was swiftly settling over us. And so I slowly forced the
letter back inside its envelope and laid it on the lawn, and
found I couldn't bring myself to say anything. I knew that it
had never been right; she was solemn and cerebral and
bound for college and I was a baseball player. Suddenly in
Anna I saw the prospect of a future that might not include
baseball, if I so chose; baseball, really, meant leaving her,
even without the hindrances of logistics and Pennsylvania
and time. What had come to pass was not a problem but a
looking glass, a mirror in which the truth emerged as solid
as a diamond. Love was too hard; it argued I could not be
my own center alone, that there were others on the planet
with me—love was impossible and too much to ask of a boy.
We sat on the lawn in the white light of the sun and Anna
insisted that distance was no object; I agreed with that, but
already I had moved farther off than she could ever realize.

"It'll work out," I told her. "It won't change anything."

But of course she knew that I lied. It was as obvious as my
shame. "I'm not going to change," she said. The words trem-
bled, the voice came softly. "I swear to it. I swear to it by
these flowers, right now."

She'd read too many books, but I didn't say that. "Swearing isn't any good," I said. "We'll just have to try to work it
out."

"But how?"

"I don't know."

"What about keeping the flowers going?"

"What about it? I'll try."

"Swear to it."

"I can't swear."

"I didn't think you could," she revealed at last. "I kind of suspected—I felt it right here." She placed her hand over her heart and held it there for a moment. "Right here. Right *here!*"

I couldn't look at her though. "Leave me alone," I said. "Okay?"

"Did I hear you correctly?" asked Anna.

"Don't talk to me," I heard myself say. "I don't love you. It doesn't have anything to do with your college or anything else. I just don't love you."

I was marveling at the blades of grass in the lawn as I spoke these words. Each molecule of each blade had taken on an unsettling, perfect clarity of being; each appeared shot through with a quiet green inner light. It seemed to me I couldn't fix myself on anything else at that moment, nothing but the texture of the lawn seemed real, and when I brought my head up at last I realized the silence had lasted too long, that Anna was no longer beside me. Something like panic overtook me in a flood and I jumped to my feet, disoriented, crazed, with just time to see her recede toward the house, recede through the flowers and then run up the porch steps, black hair streaming toward me as she turned through the door—and then Anna completely disappeared.

~~~~~~~~~~~~

Chambers turned out to be a grim and dusty town, a long, narrow street of slatternly storefronts surrounded by blocks of austere and weather-beaten homes. A kind of stasis, disquieting and ever-present, seemed to oppress the very buildings along Main Street, and nothing moved but the occasional, slow-eyed dogs who stalked their tails in the lonely shadows, stirring the dust up and eyeing everything sadly. The searing summer wind carried the aroma of sulfur from the nearby mill, and the air smelled of insecticide in the early evenings. The townspeople, like figures in a dream, moved slowly and aimlessly when they moved at all, but came to the baseball games suddenly transformed (the games were like prayer meetings or old-time revivals) and sat fanning themselves and wiping their faces on their shirt-sleeves in the bleachers, yapping in ecstasy at every base hit, swooning at every home run.

Chambers played in the Northern League, a Double A circuit that took in Saradon and Vicksburg, Oxacala and Merton, Larabee and Burris and Minapee City. The team bus rambled over roads as straight as ramrods, over pavement that sweated from a distant vantage but was only full of pockmarks and holes when you passed over it to wherever you were going. We were a team, mostly, of journeymen minor leaguers, men who had played baseball everywhere and were no longer surprised when they were traded or sold—men who played baseball for a living mechanically, with only a faint trace left of the hope they had once held inside. Some of them had had their day in the majors, of which they never spoke, and had followed a downward trajectory ever since, as though it were somehow their duty to see things through to their proper, inevitable ends. We played in dust and heat, slept on buses and in sweltering hotels, endured, with a consensual stoicism, our undeniable anonymity. I won my first start on bluster and optimism, but then I lost four badly and fell out of the rotation. Chambers used me in long relief rarely; the rest of the time I chewed gum in the bullpen, watching and wondering where I'd gone wrong.

I suppose you could say that the dream fell away then; the shell broke around me and I felt no protection in the game any longer, but only the little-known reality of it. In my room over the auto parts store on the main street of Chambers I began to have nightmares, hideous dreams in which the void of my future expressed itself as a chasm, dark and impossible to avoid. From my vantage in the bullpen the actual game seemed far away and I would daydream through whole innings, sitting forward with my elbows on my knees and my face in my hands, staring at the dusty ground. More and more I thought of the flower garden, wondered what bloomed there and what sort of birds had come to the feeders. By the time the season ended it seemed quite important—the possibility that our pink phlox had blossomed, that the candelabralike flowers of snakeroot had opened up, that perhaps the alyssum or Jacob's-coat would surprise us—the image of that lost world of color and light seemed always before me now, a salve of sorts for the wound the game had turned into.

Kansas City did not renew my contract, and I came home with baseball behind me, as if seeing the world for the first time. In my hometown the hard light of summer had softened and annealed; winds slightly cooler than summer winds blew, and in the mornings the sky appeared a heavy shade of mottled gray. I wandered a lot; at Adams Field a crowd of younger boys had come to dominate the baseball diamond, and sometimes I would sit against the chain-link fence behind the elementary school, watching their games from the hilltop. More often I would ponder the lost Eden of the flower garden, and once or twice, when night came, I passed by the hedge at the Lewis home. Beyond the clasped gate there was only darkness and the shadowy flickerings of the television in the front window, where Doctor Lewis, I knew without a doubt, looked at the late news and chewed on his cigar in the easy chair. It seemed to me that all across town the streets themselves had changed; they were narrower, the quiet in them had become a sad thing—they seemed desolate, and I saw now, improbably, that there were intricate lives in every home. *A job,* I began to say to myself, seeing how most men came out of their houses in the morning—but I couldn't bring myself, yet, to look for one. I spoke only when spoken to, and I am sure that people spoke of me as one who had failed at his dream. Yet everywhere I went I thought of our flower garden and not of baseball; perhaps, I said to myself, the day lilies have come out, or the evening primroses, or the clump of zinnias has bloomed. By the time September ended I had led myself to believe in the elusive perfection of that place, and stubbornly felt the urge to go there, to stand among the flowers one more time.

A night came in October when I awoke at two A.M. and knew the killing-frost had come. The sharp air of winter flooded at the window, and outside, illuminated by the glitter of the full moon, the leaves on the cottonwood in the yard had bound themselves up and dropped to the lawn. It dawned on me then that the flowers in our garden would close against winter now, and I got up and dressed quickly, shivering all up and down my neck and back and arms. I went out hurriedly into the street and ran toward Anna's in the cold moonlight, barreling up the old broad avenues of my paper route. When I turned into Tullis I stopped and waited while the steam of my breath died down. Moonlight bronzed everything—the leaves in the rigid maples, the clean, silent porches, the frost on the lawns and the gables and trellises—and the windowpanes all up and down the street shimmered like deep pools of water. The frost had hardened to a crust that fractured readily underfoot, and the night dew, silver in color, lay in drops the size of small pearls on the blade tips. The flowers, I thought: they will have folded up already where the frost is this thick, and I noticed uneasily a disturbance in the air then, and a steady drumming in the pit of my stomach, and my spine tightened as I walked and the tips of my ears felt furious with cold. I unclasped the gate I'd unclasped hundreds of times; inside the trimmed hedge each flagstone appeared as a ragged square of impeccable light; the three-story house rose hugely against the blue-black of the night sky, luminous, familiar, melancholy and silent—an impenetrable fortress of silver-white clapboard, with long eaves glistening beneath the moon.

Perhaps, I told myself one more time, everything will be in blossom—and then I stepped carefully along the lit flag-stones. I went through the bend in the garden path; I came on the stone bench; on the low knoll to my left and before me I saw the outline of the white gazebo. I wound through the paths and down the shadowed lawn slope, but the gar-den Anna and I had planted was only a dark mass of stems now, everything cut back to a foot in height and mulched with several inches of raked leaves from the rest of the yard.

Everything else was as it should be, as it had been, but I had no place in it anymore. I'd trespassed in order to be there at all, and suddenly I felt more alone than I ever had, more desolate, more burdened by my own soul and by who

I was, however ineluctably, and it began to seem as if my presence in that place at night beneath the moon marked the last moment ever in which I could really be young. Years have passed, but still today—on buses going downtown, in restaurants booming with noise, on airplanes as they lift off, at weddings and at movies and at baseball games when those moments arrive and the field disappears and I find myself burrowing backward in time, lost in myself as the game goes on—I have felt in my heart that same widening aloneness that buried me then: the loneliness that boys feel who are forever afraid of death and of becoming men.